GOSCINNY AND UDERZO

PRESENT

An Asterix Adventure

ASTERIX
IN
BELGIUM

Written by RENÉ GOSCINNY *and Illustrated by* ALBERT UDERZO

Translated by Anthea Bell *and* Derek Hockridge

with apologies to:
George Gordon, Lord Byron,
Mr Wm. Shakespeare, Mr John Milton
and Pieter Breughel the Elder

Asterix titles available now

1 Asterix the Gaul
2 Asterix and the Golden Sickle
3 Asterix and the Goths
4 Asterix the Gladiator
5 Asterix and the Banquet
6 Asterix and Cleopatra
7 Asterix and the Big Fight
8 Asterix in Britain
9 Asterix and the Normans
10 Asterix the Legionary
11 Asterix and the Chieftain's Shield
12 Asterix at the Olympic Games
13 Asterix and the Cauldron
14 Asterix in Spain
15 Asterix and the Roman Agent
16 Asterix in Switzerland
17 The Mansions of the Gods
18 Asterix and the Laurel Wreath
19 Asterix and the Soothsayer
20 Asterix in Corsica
21 Asterix and Caesar's Gift
22 Asterix and the Great Crossing
23 Obelix and Co.
24 Asterix in Belgium
25 Asterix and the Great Divide
26 Asterix and the Black Gold
27 Asterix and Son
28 Asterix and the Magic Carpet
29 Asterix and the Secret Weapon
30 Asterix and Obelix All at Sea
31 Asterix and the Actress
32 Asterix and the Class Act
33 Asterix and the Falling Sky
34 Asterix and Obelix's Birthday – the Golden Book
35 Asterix and the Picts
Where's Asterix?
Where's Dogmatix?
Asterix and the Vikings
Asterix at the Olympic Games (film tie-in)
Asterix Omnibus 1 (Books 1-3)
Asterix Omnibus 2 (Books 4-6)
Asterix Omnibus 3 (Books 7-9)
Asterix Omnibus 4 (Books 10-12)
Asterix Omnibus 5 (Books 13-15)
Asterix Omnibus 6 (Books 16-18)
Asterix Omnibus 7 (Books 19-21)
Asterix Omnibus 8 (Books 22-24)
Asterix Omnibus 9 (Books 25-27)
Asterix Omnibus 10 (Books 28-30)
Asterix Omnibus 11 (Books 31-33)
How Obelix Fell into the Magic Potion

Original title: *Astérix chez les Belges*

Exclusive licensee: Orion Publishing Group
Translators: Anthea Bell and Derek Hockridge
Typography: Bryony Newhouse

This revised edition first published in 2004 by Orion Books Ltd,
Orion House, 5 Upper St Martin's Lane, London WC2H 9EA
An Hachette UK company

13 15 17 19 20 18 16 14

Printed in China

www.asterix.com
www.orionbooks.co.uk

A CIP record for this book is available from the British Library

ISBN 978-0-7528-6649-9 (cased)
ISBN 978-0-7528-6650-5 (paperback)
ISBN 978-1-4440-1331-3 (ebook)

The Orion Publishing Group's policy is to use papers that are natural, renewable and recyclable products and made from wood grown in sustainable forests. The logging and manufacturing processes are expected to conform to the environmental regulations of the country of origin.

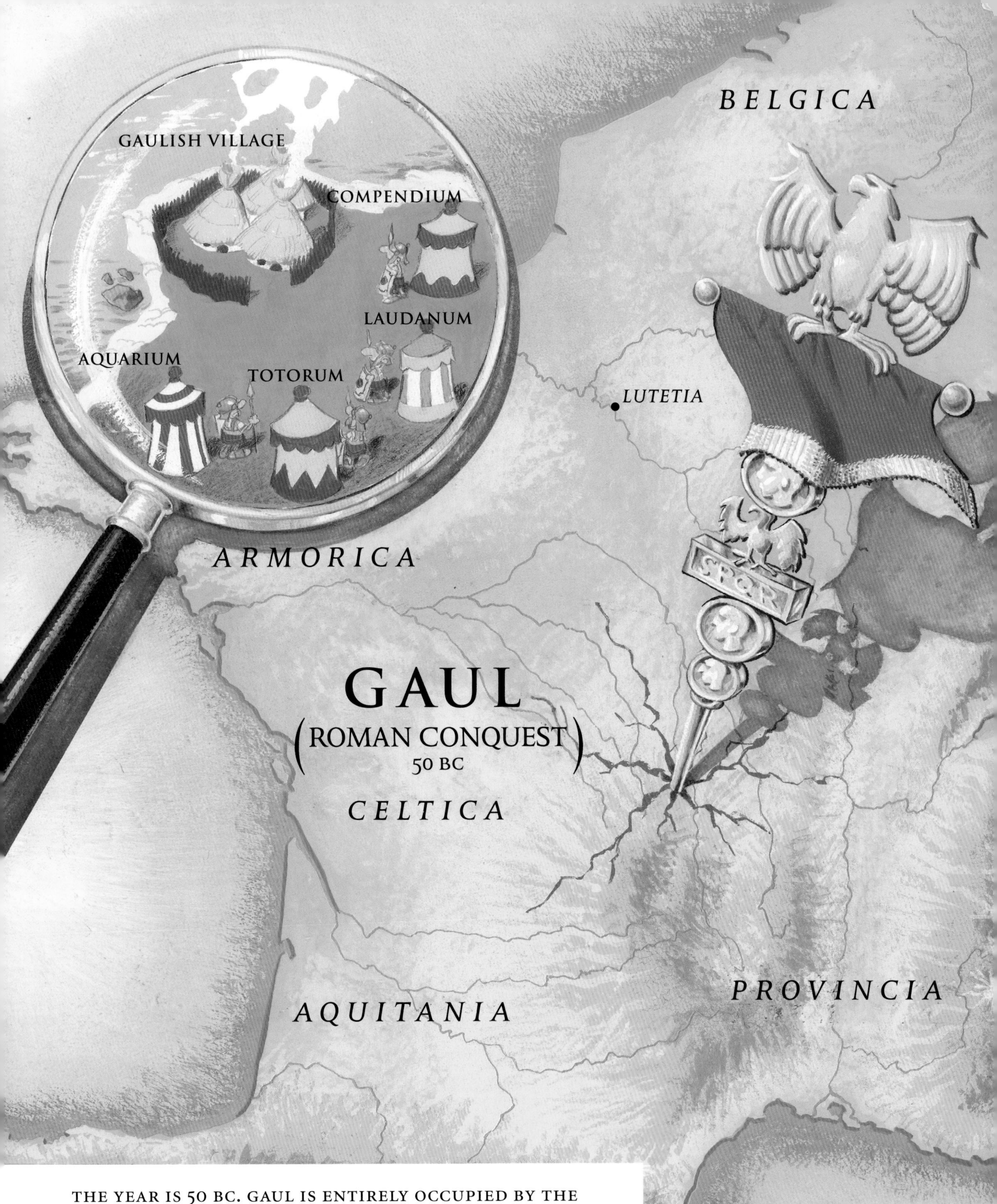
BELGICA
GAULISH VILLAGE
COMPENDIUM
LAUDANUM
AQUARIUM
TOTORUM
LUTETIA
SPQR
ARMORICA
GAUL
(ROMAN CONQUEST)
50 BC
CELTICA
AQUITANIA
PROVINCIA

THE YEAR IS 50 BC. GAUL IS ENTIRELY OCCUPIED BY THE ROMANS. WELL, NOT ENTIRELY ... ONE SMALL VILLAGE OF INDOMITABLE GAULS STILL HOLDS OUT AGAINST THE INVADERS. AND LIFE IS NOT EASY FOR THE ROMAN LEGIONARIES WHO GARRISON THE FORTIFIED CAMPS OF TOTORUM, AQUARIUM, LAUDANUM AND COMPENDIUM ...

ASTERIX, THE HERO OF THESE ADVENTURES. A SHREWD, CUNNING LITTLE WARRIOR, ALL PERILOUS MISSIONS ARE IMMEDIATELY ENTRUSTED TO HIM. ASTERIX GETS HIS SUPERHUMAN STRENGTH FROM THE MAGIC POTION BREWED BY THE DRUID GETAFIX . . .

OBELIX, ASTERIX'S INSEPARABLE FRIEND. A MENHIR DELIVERY MAN BY TRADE, ADDICTED TO WILD BOAR. OBELIX IS ALWAYS READY TO DROP EVERYTHING AND GO OFF ON A NEW ADVENTURE WITH ASTERIX – SO LONG AS THERE'S WILD BOAR TO EAT, AND PLENTY OF FIGHTING. HIS CONSTANT COMPANION IS DOGMATIX, THE ONLY KNOWN CANINE ECOLOGIST, WHO HOWLS WITH DESPAIR WHEN A TREE IS CUT DOWN.

GETAFIX, THE VENERABLE VILLAGE DRUID, GATHERS MISTLETOE AND BREWS MAGIC POTIONS. HIS SPECIALITY IS THE POTION WHICH GIVES THE DRINKER SUPERHUMAN STRENGTH. BUT GETAFIX ALSO HAS OTHER RECIPES UP HIS SLEEVE . . .

CACOFONIX, THE BARD. OPINION IS DIVIDED AS TO HIS MUSICAL GIFTS. CACOFONIX THINKS HE'S A GENIUS. EVERY-ONE ELSE THINKS HE'S UNSPEAKABLE. BUT SO LONG AS HE DOESN'T SPEAK, LET ALONE SING, EVERYBODY LIKES HIM . . .

FINALLY, VITALSTATISTIX, THE CHIEF OF THE TRIBE. MAJESTIC, BRAVE AND HOT-TEMPERED, THE OLD WARRIOR IS RESPECTED BY HIS MEN AND FEARED BY HIS ENEMIES. VITALSTATISTIX HIMSELF HAS ONLY ONE FEAR, HE IS AFRAID THE SKY MAY FALL ON HIS HEAD TOMORROW. BUT AS HE ALWAYS SAYS, TOMORROW NEVER COMES.

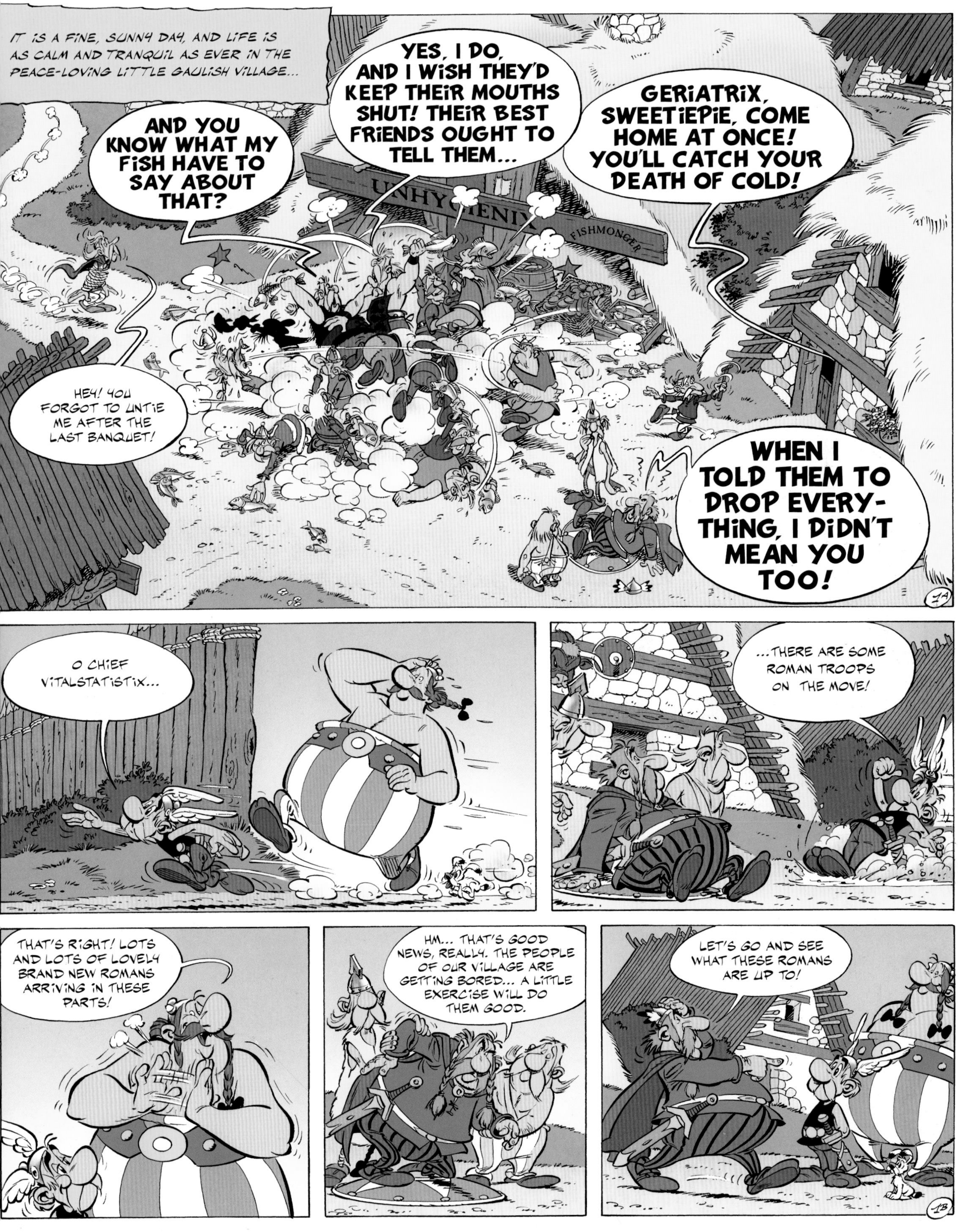
IT IS A FINE, SUNNY DAY, AND LIFE IS AS CALM AND TRANQUIL AS EVER IN THE PEACE-LOVING LITTLE GAULISH VILLAGE...
AND YOU KNOW WHAT MY FISH HAVE TO SAY ABOUT THAT?
YES, I DO, AND I WISH THEY'D KEEP THEIR MOUTHS SHUT! THEIR BEST FRIENDS OUGHT TO TELL THEM...
GERIATRIX, SWEETIEPIE, COME HOME AT ONCE! YOU'LL CATCH YOUR DEATH OF COLD!
UNHYGIENIX
FISHMONGER
HEY! YOU FORGOT TO UNTIE ME AFTER THE LAST BANQUET!
WHEN I TOLD THEM TO DROP EVERY-THING, I DIDN'T MEAN YOU TOO!
O CHIEF VITALSTATISTIX...
...THERE ARE SOME ROMAN TROOPS ON THE MOVE!
THAT'S RIGHT! LOTS AND LOTS OF LOVELY BRAND NEW ROMANS ARRIVING IN THESE PARTS!
HM... THAT'S GOOD NEWS, REALLY. THE PEOPLE OF OUR VILLAGE ARE GETTING BORED... A LITTLE EXERCISE WILL DO THEM GOOD.
LET'S GO AND SEE WHAT THESE ROMANS ARE UP TO!

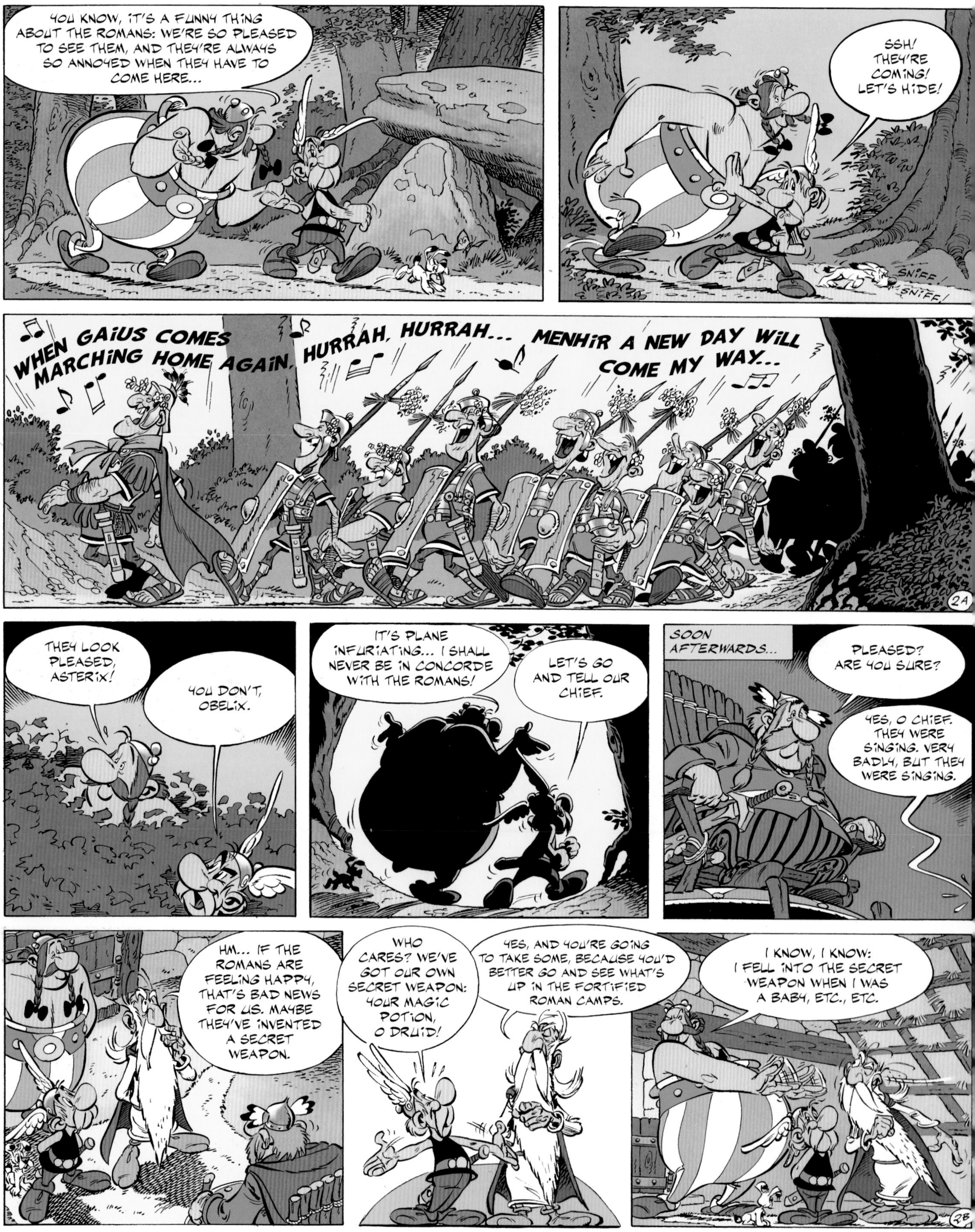

YOU KNOW, IT'S A FUNNY THING ABOUT THE ROMANS: WE'RE SO PLEASED TO SEE THEM, AND THEY'RE ALWAYS SO ANNOYED WHEN THEY HAVE TO COME HERE...
SSH! THEY'RE COMING! LET'S HIDE!
SNIFF! SNIFF!
WHEN GAIUS COMES MARCHING HOME AGAIN, HURRAH, HURRAH... MENHIR A NEW DAY WILL COME MY WAY...
2A
THEY LOOK PLEASED, ASTERIX!
YOU DON'T, OBELIX.
IT'S PLANE INFURIATING... I SHALL NEVER BE IN CONCORDE WITH THE ROMANS!
LET'S GO AND TELL OUR CHIEF.
SOON AFTERWARDS...
PLEASED? ARE YOU SURE?
YES, O CHIEF. THEY WERE SINGING. VERY BADLY, BUT THEY WERE SINGING.
HM... IF THE ROMANS ARE FEELING HAPPY, THAT'S BAD NEWS FOR US. MAYBE THEY'VE INVENTED A SECRET WEAPON.
WHO CARES? WE'VE GOT OUR OWN SECRET WEAPON: YOUR MAGIC POTION, O DRUID!
YES, AND YOU'RE GOING TO TAKE SOME, BECAUSE YOU'D BETTER GO AND SEE WHAT'S UP IN THE FORTIFIED ROMAN CAMPS.
I KNOW, I KNOW: I FELL INTO THE SECRET WEAPON WHEN I WAS A BABY, ETC., ETC.
2B

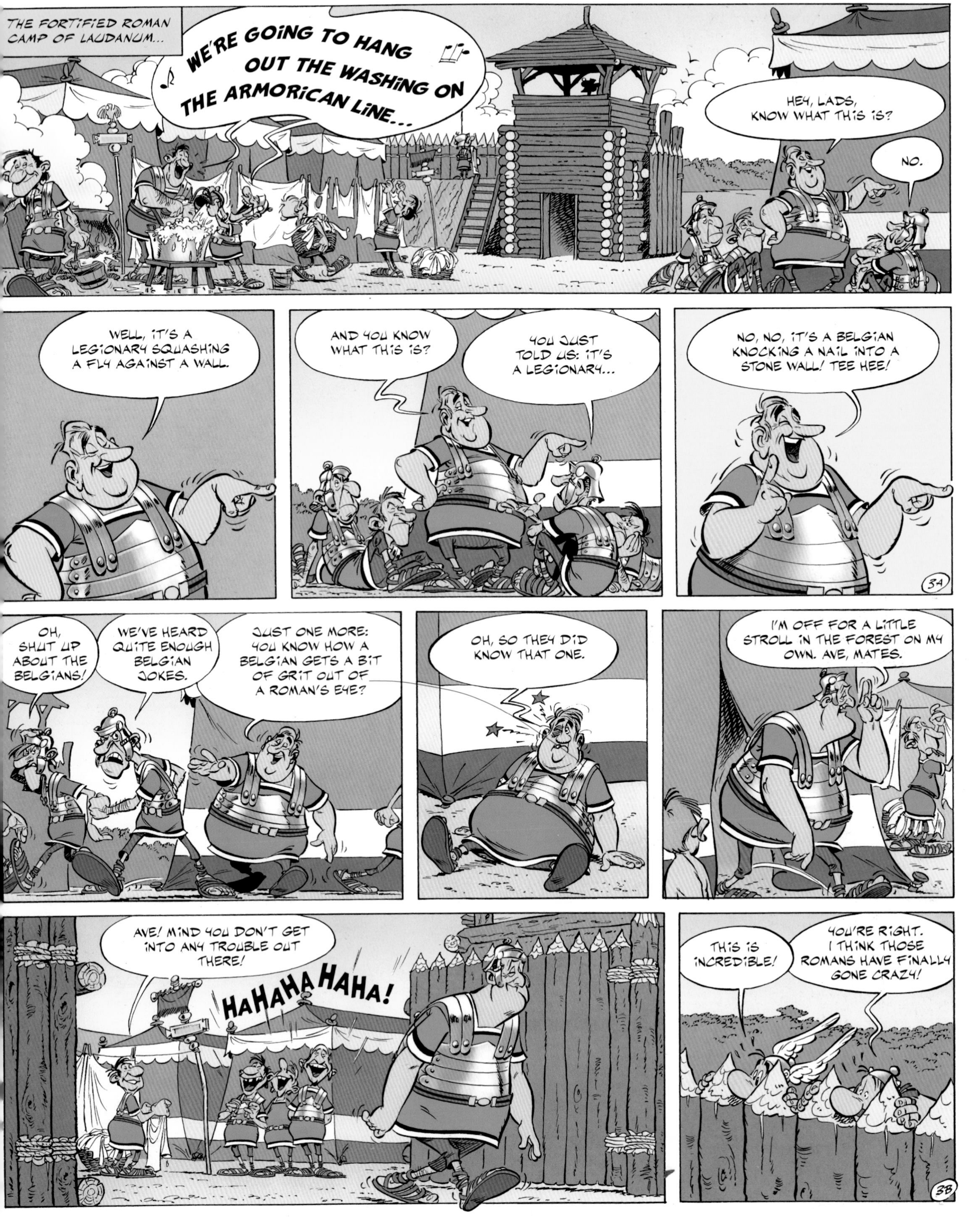

THE FORTIFIED ROMAN CAMP OF LAUDANUM...
WE'RE GOING TO HANG OUT THE WASHING ON THE ARMORICAN LINE...
HEY, LADS, KNOW WHAT THIS IS?
NO.
WELL, IT'S A LEGIONARY SQUASHING A FLY AGAINST A WALL.
AND YOU KNOW WHAT THIS IS?
YOU JUST TOLD US: IT'S A LEGIONARY...
NO, NO, IT'S A BELGIAN KNOCKING A NAIL INTO A STONE WALL! TEE HEE!
OH, SHUT UP ABOUT THE BELGIANS!
WE'VE HEARD QUITE ENOUGH BELGIAN JOKES.
JUST ONE MORE: YOU KNOW HOW A BELGIAN GETS A BIT OF GRIT OUT OF A ROMAN'S EYE?
OH, SO THEY DID KNOW THAT ONE.
I'M OFF FOR A LITTLE STROLL IN THE FOREST ON MY OWN. AVE, MATES.
AVE! MIND YOU DON'T GET INTO ANY TROUBLE OUT THERE!
HAHAHAHAHA!
THIS IS INCREDIBLE!
YOU'RE RIGHT. I THINK THOSE ROMANS HAVE FINALLY GONE CRAZY!

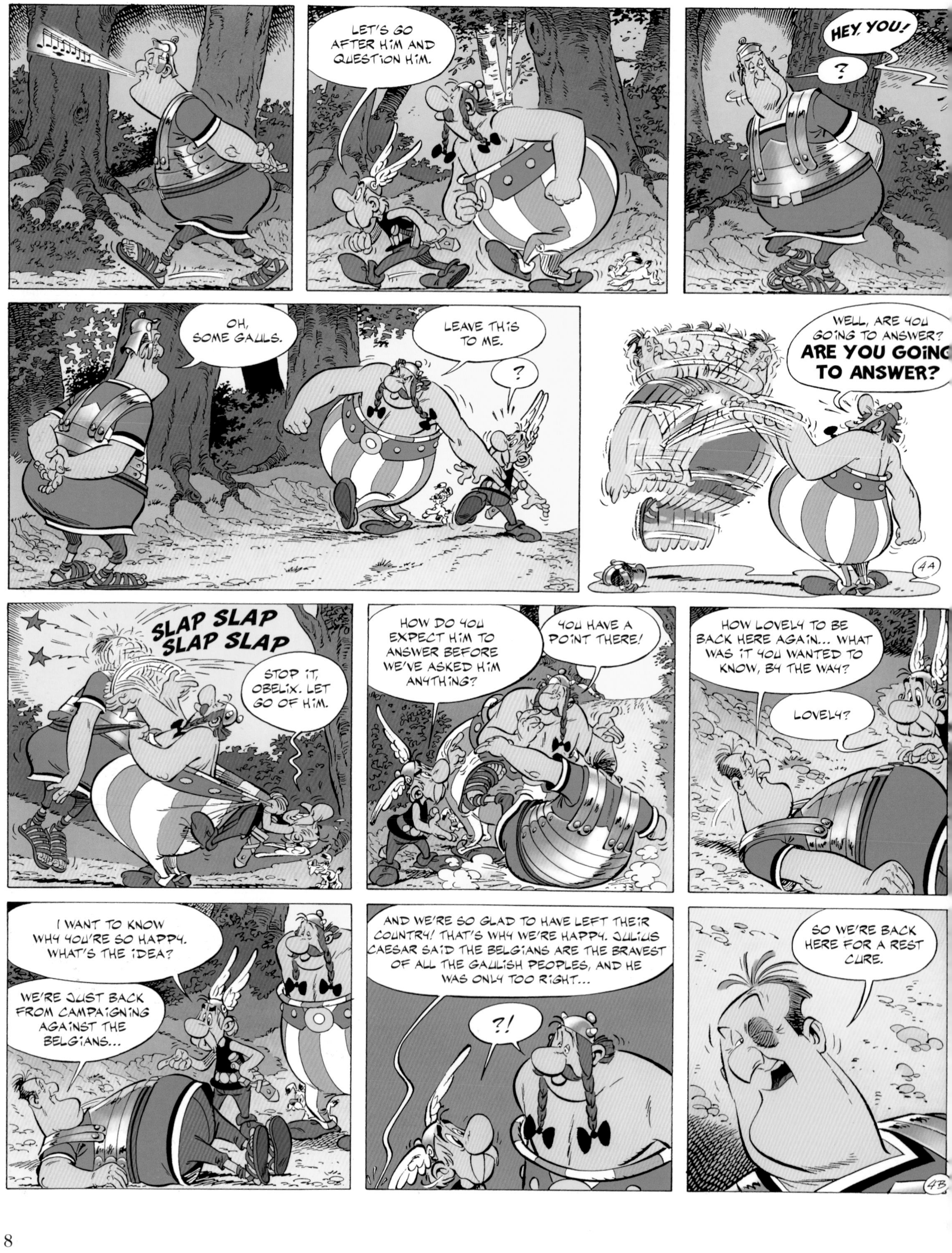
LET'S GO AFTER HIM AND QUESTION HIM.
HEY, YOU!
?
OH, SOME GAULS.
LEAVE THIS TO ME.
?
WELL, ARE YOU GOING TO ANSWER? ARE YOU GOING TO ANSWER?
SLAP SLAP SLAP SLAP
STOP IT, OBELIX. LET GO OF HIM.
HOW DO YOU EXPECT HIM TO ANSWER BEFORE WE'VE ASKED HIM ANYTHING?
YOU HAVE A POINT THERE!
HOW LOVELY TO BE BACK HERE AGAIN... WHAT WAS IT YOU WANTED TO KNOW, BY THE WAY?
LOVELY?
I WANT TO KNOW WHY YOU'RE SO HAPPY. WHAT'S THE IDEA?
WE'RE JUST BACK FROM CAMPAIGNING AGAINST THE BELGIANS...
AND WE'RE SO GLAD TO HAVE LEFT THEIR COUNTRY! THAT'S WHY WE'RE HAPPY. JULIUS CAESAR SAID THE BELGIANS ARE THE BRAVEST OF ALL THE GAULISH PEOPLES, AND HE WAS ONLY TOO RIGHT...
?!
SO WE'RE BACK HERE FOR A REST CURE.

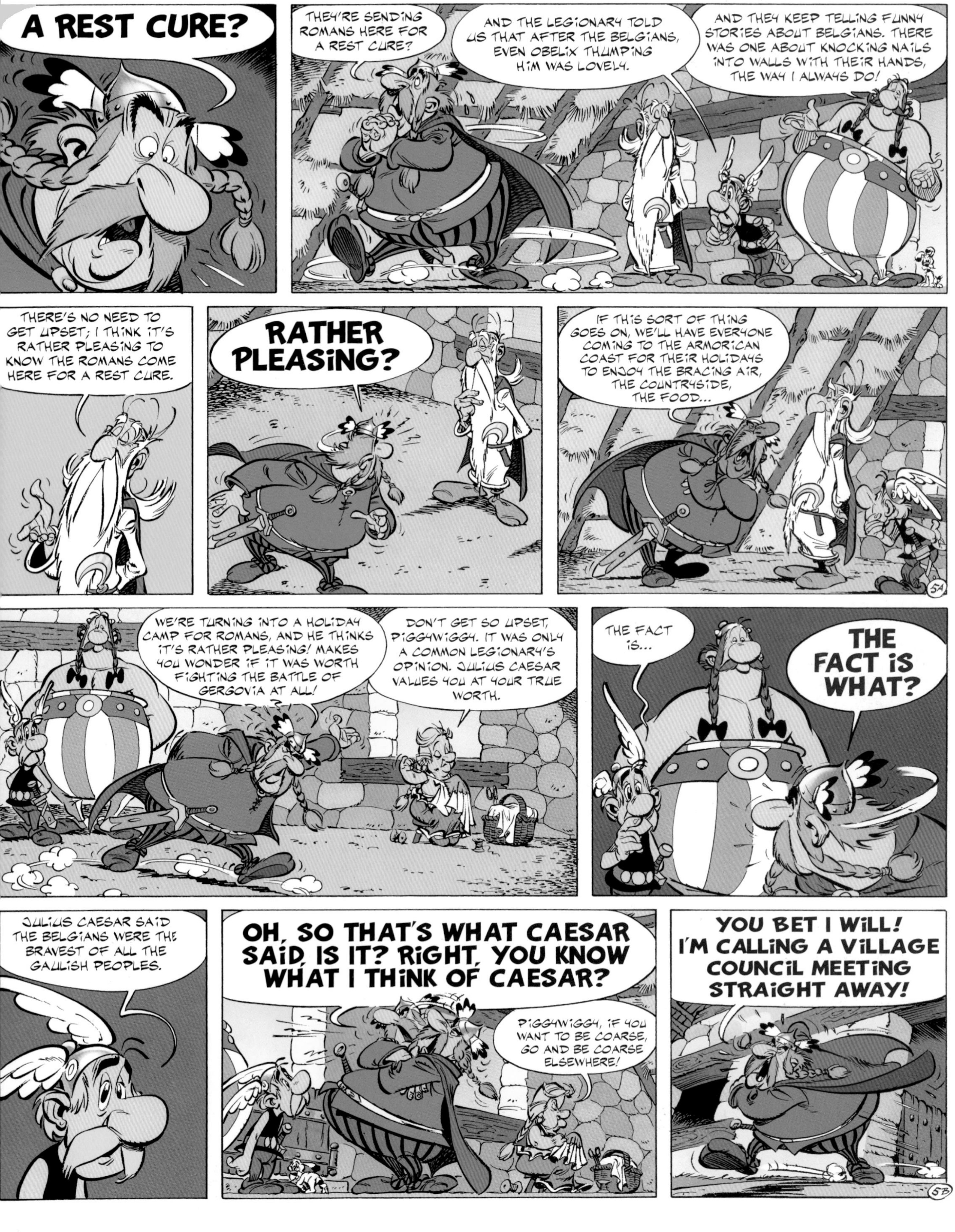
A REST CURE?
THEY'RE SENDING ROMANS HERE FOR A REST CURE?
AND THE LEGIONARY TOLD US THAT AFTER THE BELGIANS, EVEN OBELIX THUMPING HIM WAS LOVELY.
AND THEY KEEP TELLING FUNNY STORIES ABOUT BELGIANS. THERE WAS ONE ABOUT KNOCKING NAILS INTO WALLS WITH THEIR HANDS, THE WAY I ALWAYS DO!
THERE'S NO NEED TO GET UPSET; I THINK IT'S RATHER PLEASING TO KNOW THE ROMANS COME HERE FOR A REST CURE.
RATHER PLEASING?
IF THIS SORT OF THING GOES ON, WE'LL HAVE EVERYONE COMING TO THE ARMORICAN COAST FOR THEIR HOLIDAYS TO ENJOY THE BRACING AIR, THE COUNTRYSIDE, THE FOOD...
WE'RE TURNING INTO A HOLIDAY CAMP FOR ROMANS, AND HE THINKS IT'S RATHER PLEASING! MAKES YOU WONDER IF IT WAS WORTH FIGHTING THE BATTLE OF GERGOVIA AT ALL!
DON'T GET SO UPSET, PIGGYWIGGY. IT WAS ONLY A COMMON LEGIONARY'S OPINION. JULIUS CAESAR VALUES YOU AT YOUR TRUE WORTH.
THE FACT IS...
THE FACT IS WHAT?
JULIUS CAESAR SAID THE BELGIANS WERE THE BRAVEST OF ALL THE GAULISH PEOPLES.
OH, SO THAT'S WHAT CAESAR SAID, IS IT? RIGHT, YOU KNOW WHAT I THINK OF CAESAR?
PIGGYWIGGY, IF YOU WANT TO BE COARSE, GO AND BE COARSE ELSEWHERE!
YOU BET I WILL! I'M CALLING A VILLAGE COUNCIL MEETING STRAIGHT AWAY!

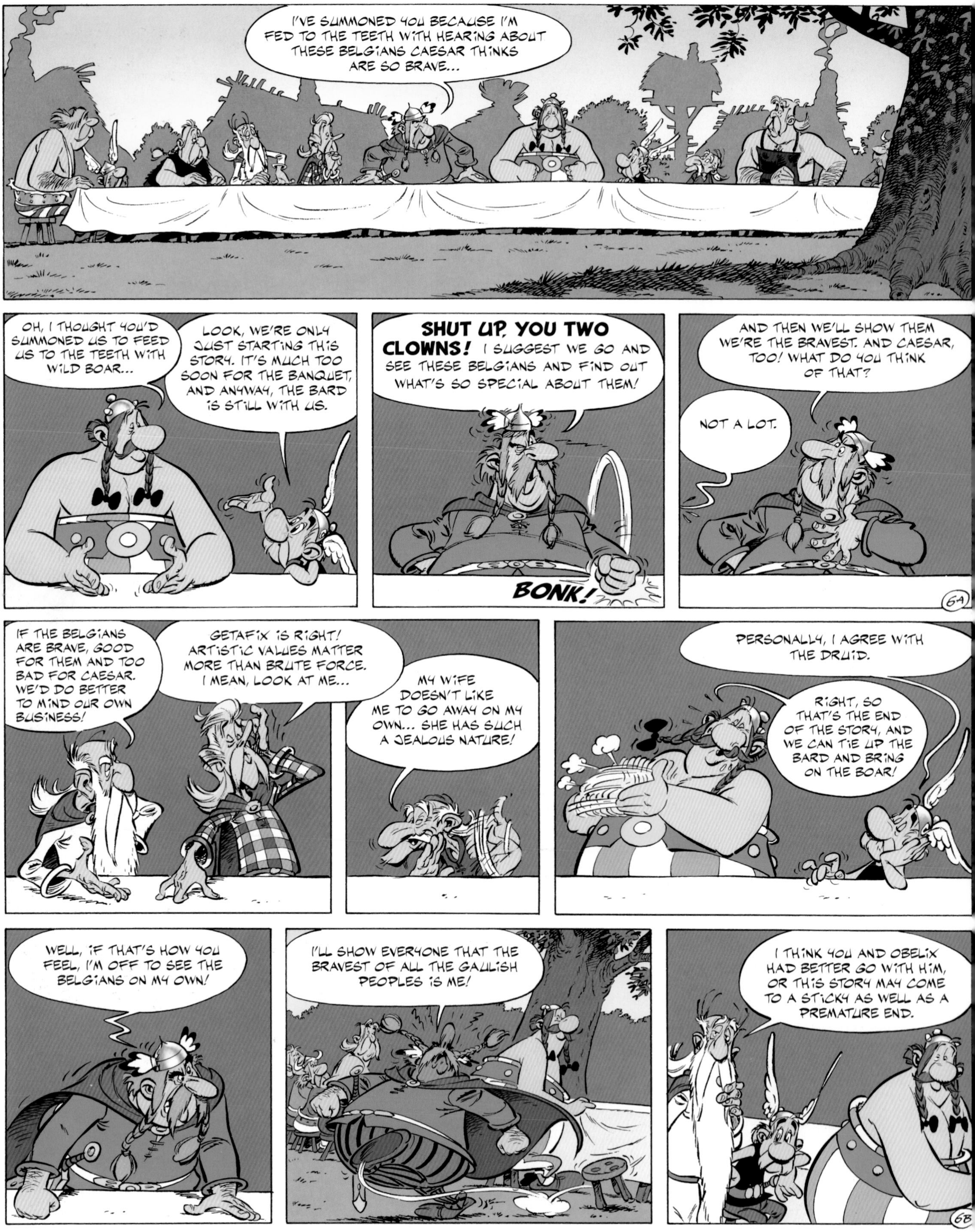
I'VE SUMMONED YOU BECAUSE I'M FED TO THE TEETH WITH HEARING ABOUT THESE BELGIANS CAESAR THINKS ARE SO BRAVE...
OH, I THOUGHT YOU'D SUMMONED US TO FEED US TO THE TEETH WITH WILD BOAR...
LOOK, WE'RE ONLY JUST STARTING THIS STORY. IT'S MUCH TOO SOON FOR THE BANQUET, AND ANYWAY, THE BARD IS STILL WITH US.
SHUT UP, YOU TWO CLOWNS! I SUGGEST WE GO AND SEE THESE BELGIANS AND FIND OUT WHAT'S SO SPECIAL ABOUT THEM!
BONK!
AND THEN WE'LL SHOW THEM WE'RE THE BRAVEST. AND CAESAR, TOO! WHAT DO YOU THINK OF THAT?
NOT A LOT.
IF THE BELGIANS ARE BRAVE, GOOD FOR THEM AND TOO BAD FOR CAESAR. WE'D DO BETTER TO MIND OUR OWN BUSINESS!
GETAFIX IS RIGHT! ARTISTIC VALUES MATTER MORE THAN BRUTE FORCE. I MEAN, LOOK AT ME...
MY WIFE DOESN'T LIKE ME TO GO AWAY ON MY OWN... SHE HAS SUCH A JEALOUS NATURE!
PERSONALLY, I AGREE WITH THE DRUID.
RIGHT, SO THAT'S THE END OF THE STORY, AND WE CAN TIE UP THE BARD AND BRING ON THE BOAR!
WELL, IF THAT'S HOW YOU FEEL, I'M OFF TO SEE THE BELGIANS ON MY OWN!
I'LL SHOW EVERYONE THAT THE BRAVEST OF ALL THE GAULISH PEOPLES IS ME!
I THINK YOU AND OBELIX HAD BETTER GO WITH HIM, OR THIS STORY MAY COME TO A STICKY AS WELL AS A PREMATURE END.

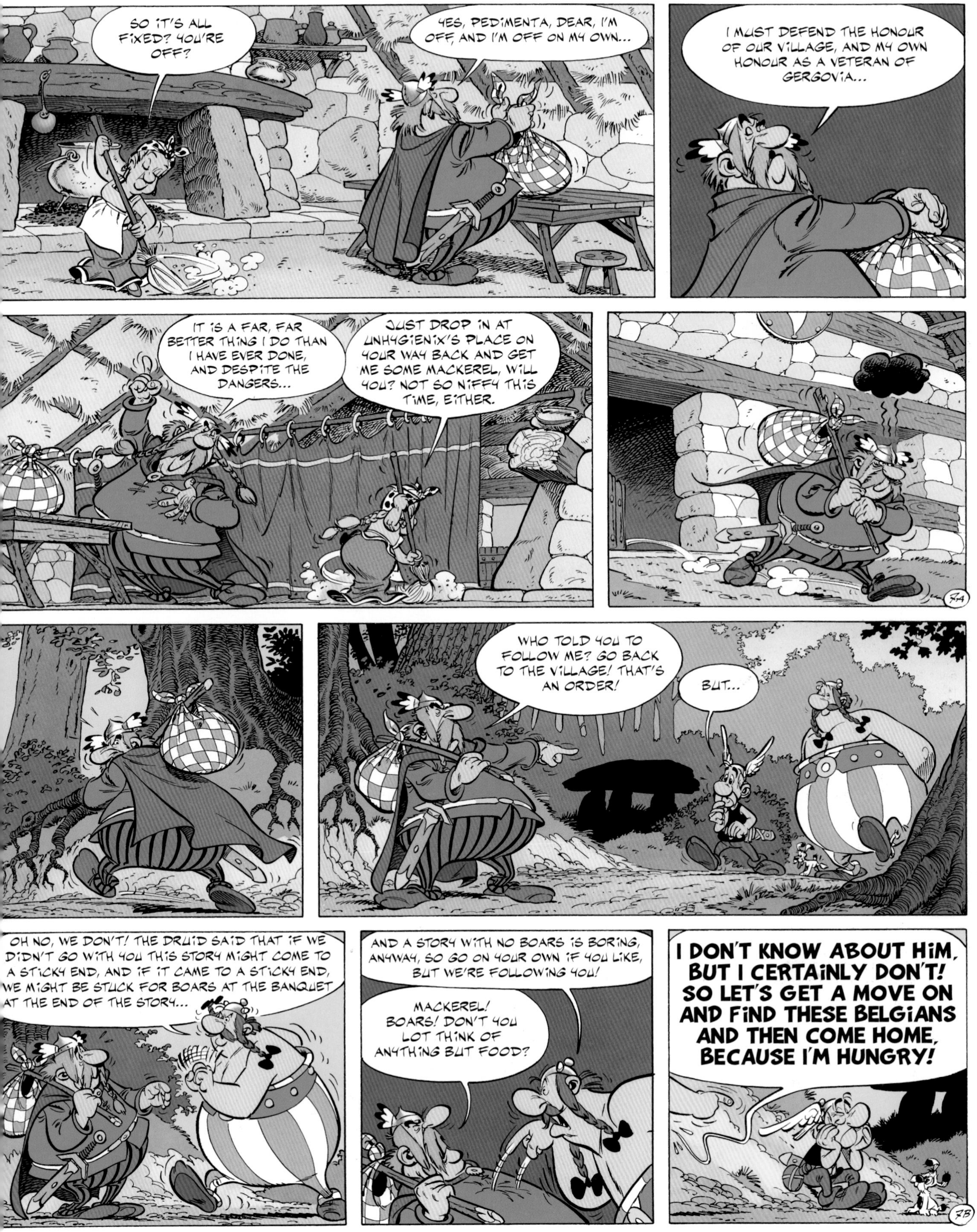
SO IT'S ALL FIXED? YOU'RE OFF?
YES, PEDIMENTA, DEAR, I'M OFF, AND I'M OFF ON MY OWN...
I MUST DEFEND THE HONOUR OF OUR VILLAGE, AND MY OWN HONOUR AS A VETERAN OF GERGOVIA...
IT IS A FAR, FAR BETTER THING I DO THAN I HAVE EVER DONE, AND DESPITE THE DANGERS...
JUST DROP IN AT UNHYGIENIX'S PLACE ON YOUR WAY BACK AND GET ME SOME MACKEREL, WILL YOU? NOT SO NIFFY THIS TIME, EITHER.
WHO TOLD YOU TO FOLLOW ME? GO BACK TO THE VILLAGE! THAT'S AN ORDER!
BUT...
OH NO, WE DON'T! THE DRUID SAID THAT IF WE DIDN'T GO WITH YOU THIS STORY MIGHT COME TO A STICKY END, AND IF IT CAME TO A STICKY END, WE MIGHT BE STUCK FOR BOARS AT THE BANQUET AT THE END OF THE STORY...
AND A STORY WITH NO BOARS IS BORING, ANYWAY, SO GO ON YOUR OWN IF YOU LIKE, BUT WE'RE FOLLOWING YOU!
MACKEREL! BOARS! DON'T YOU LOT THINK OF ANYTHING BUT FOOD?
I DON'T KNOW ABOUT HIM, BUT I CERTAINLY DON'T! SO LET'S GET A MOVE ON AND FIND THESE BELGIANS AND THEN COME HOME, BECAUSE I'M HUNGRY!

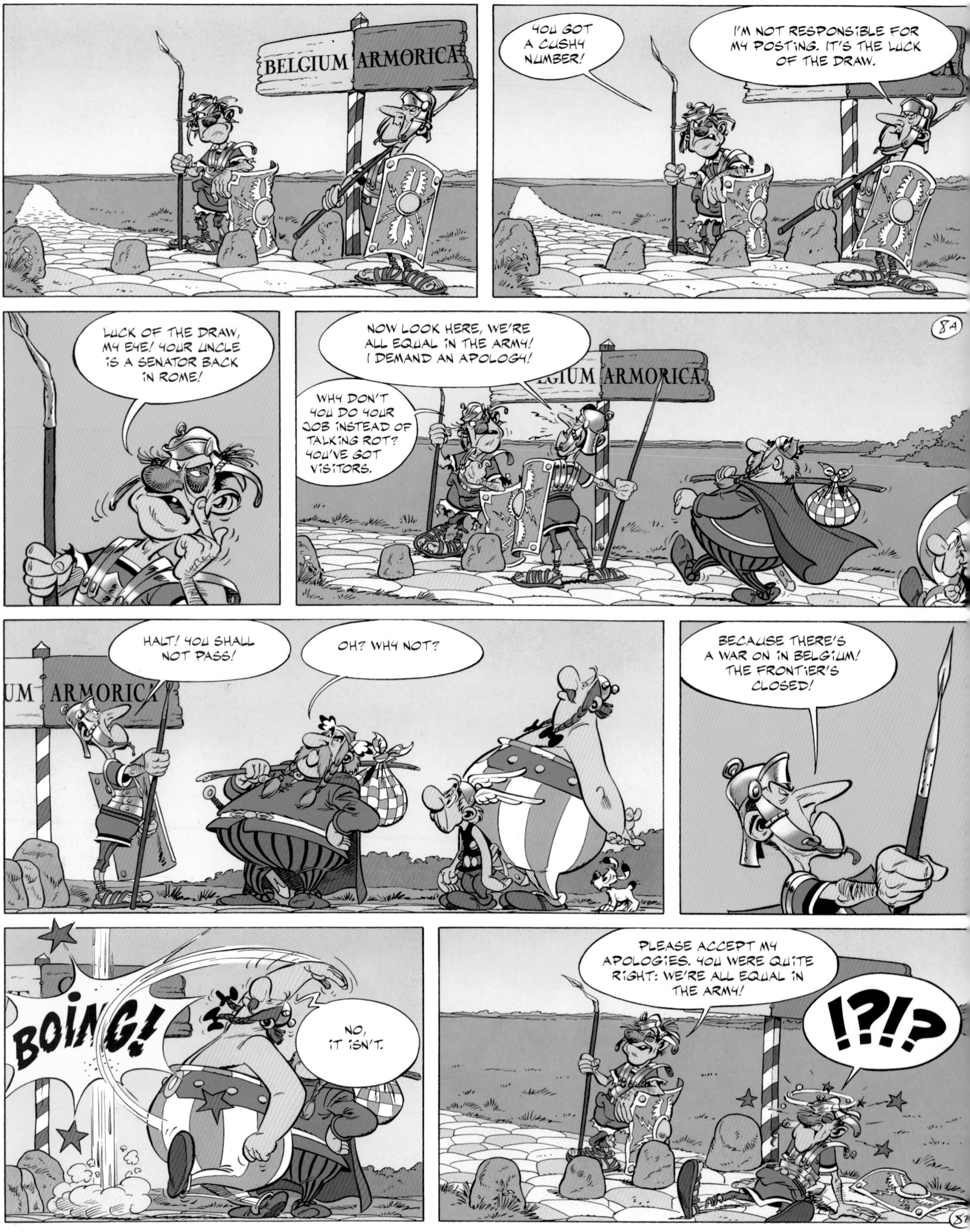
BELGIUM
ARMORICA
YOU GOT A CUSHY NUMBER!
I'M NOT RESPONSIBLE FOR MY POSTING. IT'S THE LUCK OF THE DRAW.
LUCK OF THE DRAW, MY EYE! YOUR UNCLE IS A SENATOR BACK IN ROME!
NOW LOOK HERE, WE'RE ALL EQUAL IN THE ARMY! I DEMAND AN APOLOGY!
WHY DON'T YOU DO YOUR JOB INSTEAD OF TALKING ROT? YOU'VE GOT VISITORS.
HALT! YOU SHALL NOT PASS!
OH? WHY NOT?
BECAUSE THERE'S A WAR ON IN BELGIUM! THE FRONTIER'S CLOSED!
BOING!
NO, IT ISN'T.
PLEASE ACCEPT MY APOLOGIES. YOU WERE QUITE RIGHT: WE'RE ALL EQUAL IN THE ARMY!
!?!?

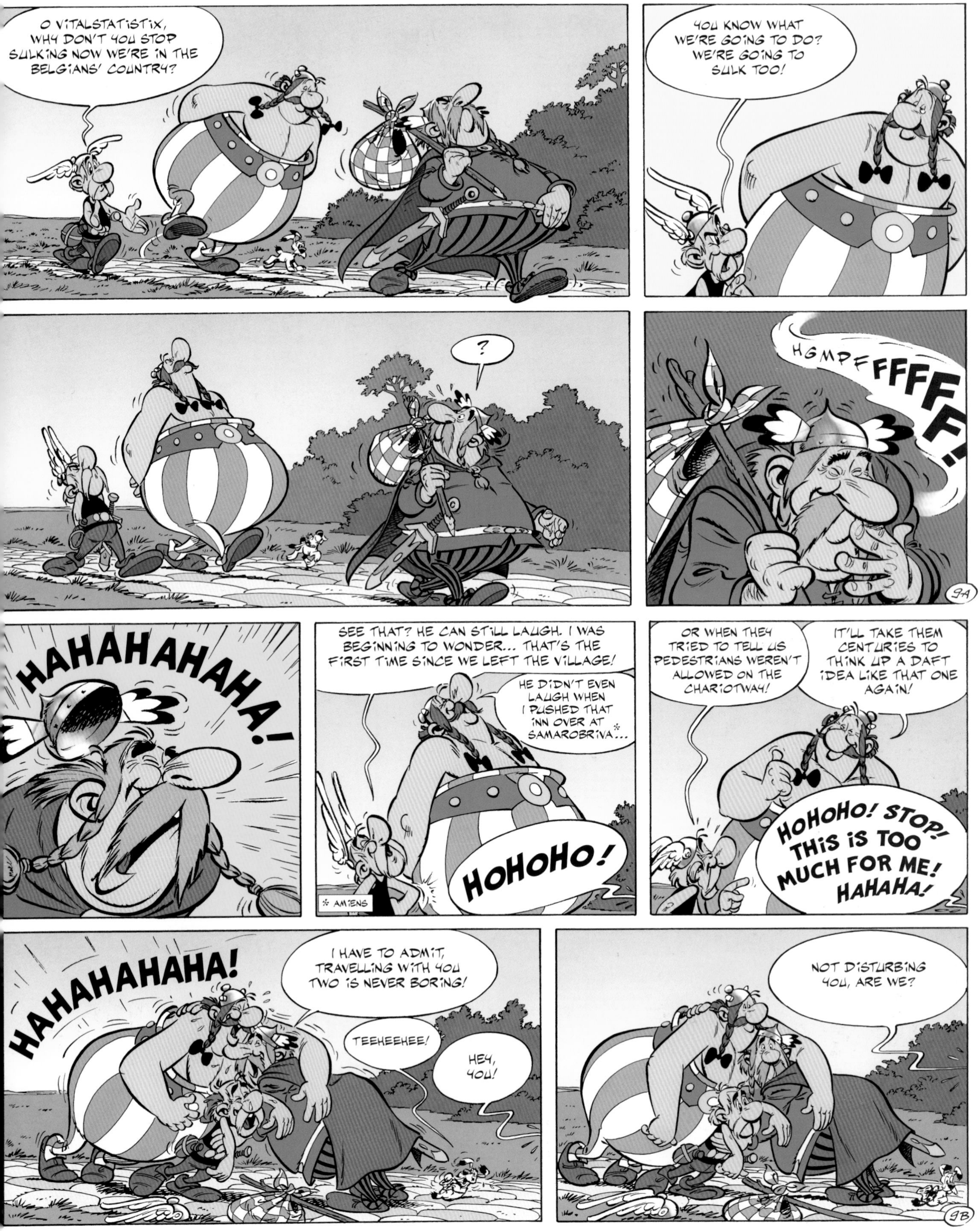

O VITALSTATISTIX, WHY DON'T YOU STOP SULKING NOW WE'RE IN THE BELGIANS' COUNTRY?
YOU KNOW WHAT WE'RE GOING TO DO? WE'RE GOING TO SULK TOO!
?
HGMPFFFFFF!
HAHAHAHAHAHA!
SEE THAT? HE CAN STILL LAUGH. I WAS BEGINNING TO WONDER... THAT'S THE FIRST TIME SINCE WE LEFT THE VILLAGE!
HE DIDN'T EVEN LAUGH WHEN I PUSHED THAT INN OVER AT SAMAROBRIVA*...
HOHOHO!
* AMIENS
OR WHEN THEY TRIED TO TELL US PEDESTRIANS WEREN'T ALLOWED ON THE CHARIOTWAY!
IT'LL TAKE THEM CENTURIES TO THINK UP A DAFT IDEA LIKE THAT ONE AGAIN!
HOHOHO! STOP! THIS IS TOO MUCH FOR ME! HAHAHA!
HAHAHAHAHA!
I HAVE TO ADMIT, TRAVELLING WITH YOU TWO IS NEVER BORING!
TEEHEEHEE!
HEY, YOU!
NOT DISTURBING YOU, ARE WE?

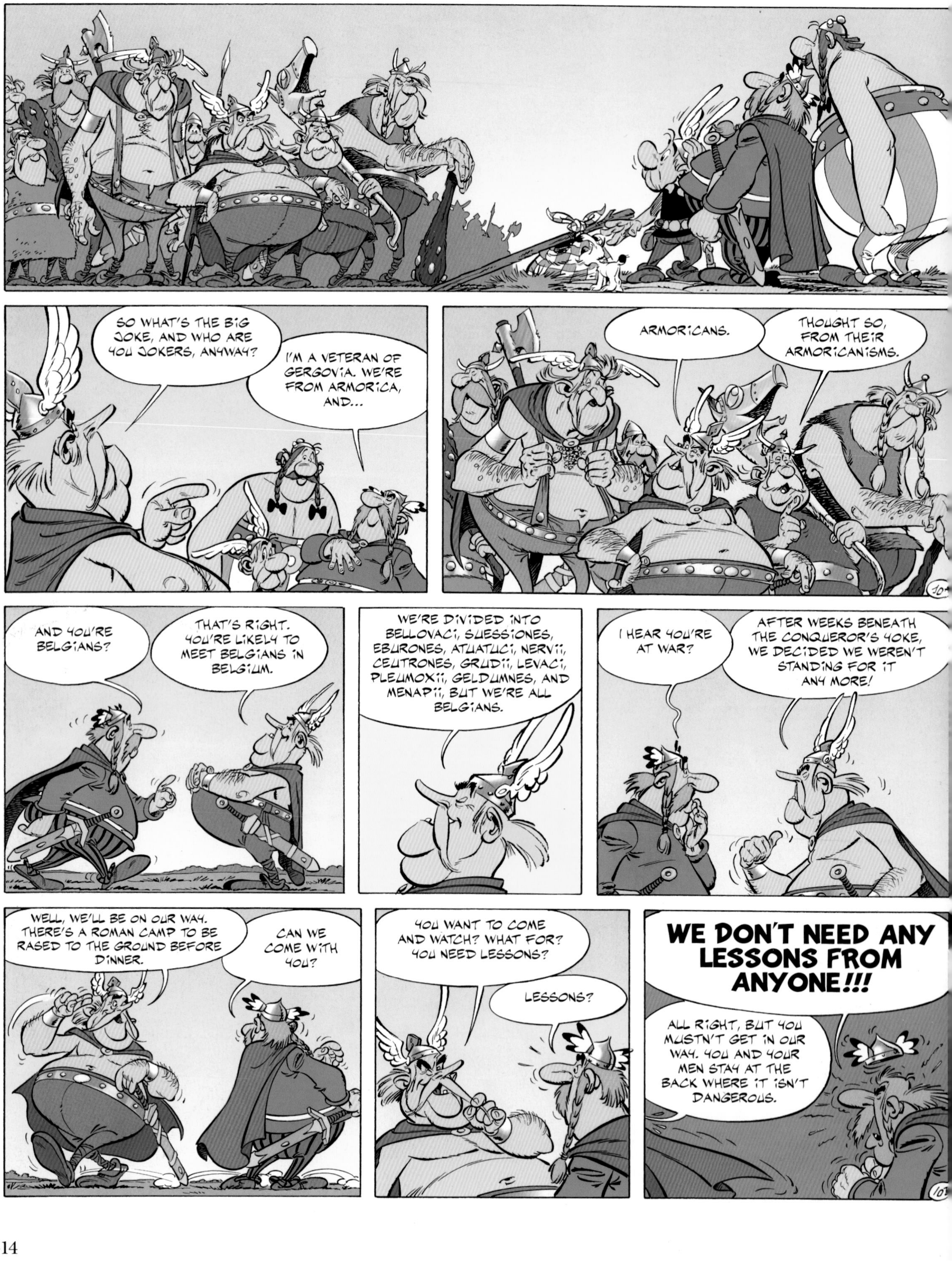
SO WHAT'S THE BIG JOKE, AND WHO ARE YOU JOKERS, ANYWAY?
I'M A VETERAN OF GERGOVIA. WE'RE FROM ARMORICA, AND...
ARMORICANS.
THOUGHT SO, FROM THEIR ARMORICANISMS.
AND YOU'RE BELGIANS?
THAT'S RIGHT. YOU'RE LIKELY TO MEET BELGIANS IN BELGIUM.
WE'RE DIVIDED INTO BELLOVACI, SUESSIONES, EBURONES, ATUATUCI, NERVII, CEUTRONES, GRUDII, LEVACI, PLEUMOXII, GELDUMNES, AND MENAPII, BUT WE'RE ALL BELGIANS.
I HEAR YOU'RE AT WAR?
AFTER WEEKS BENEATH THE CONQUEROR'S YOKE, WE DECIDED WE WEREN'T STANDING FOR IT ANY MORE!
WELL, WE'LL BE ON OUR WAY. THERE'S A ROMAN CAMP TO BE RASED TO THE GROUND BEFORE DINNER.
CAN WE COME WITH YOU?
YOU WANT TO COME AND WATCH? WHAT FOR? YOU NEED LESSONS?
LESSONS?
WE DON'T NEED ANY LESSONS FROM ANYONE!!!
ALL RIGHT, BUT YOU MUSTN'T GET IN OUR WAY. YOU AND YOUR MEN STAY AT THE BACK WHERE IT ISN'T DANGEROUS.

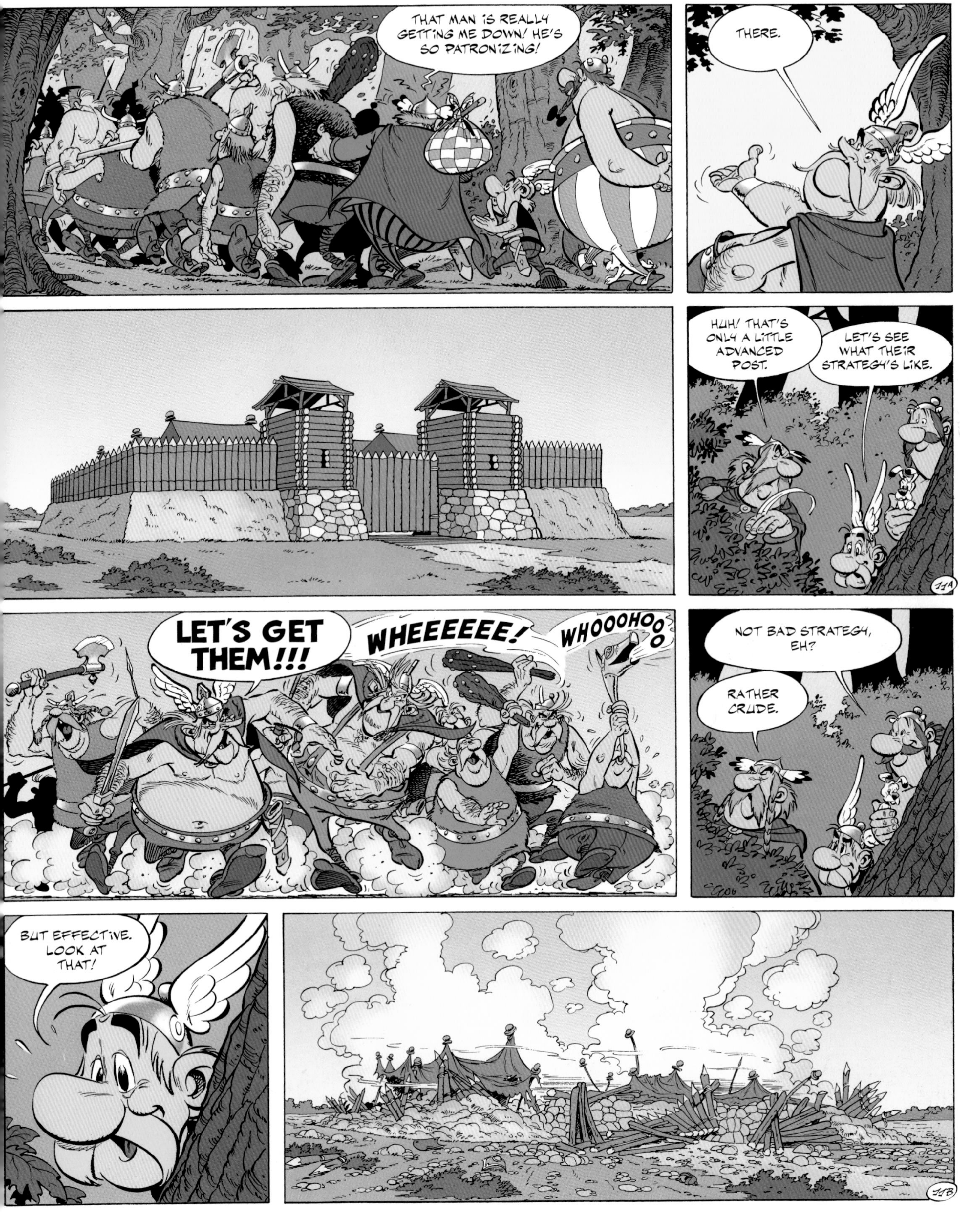

THAT MAN IS REALLY GETTING ME DOWN! HE'S SO PATRONIZING!
THERE.
HUH! THAT'S ONLY A LITTLE ADVANCED POST.
LET'S SEE WHAT THEIR STRATEGY'S LIKE.
11A
LET'S GET THEM!!!
WHEEEEEE!
WHOOOHOOO
NOT BAD STRATEGY, EH?
RATHER CRUDE.
BUT EFFECTIVE. LOOK AT THAT!
11B

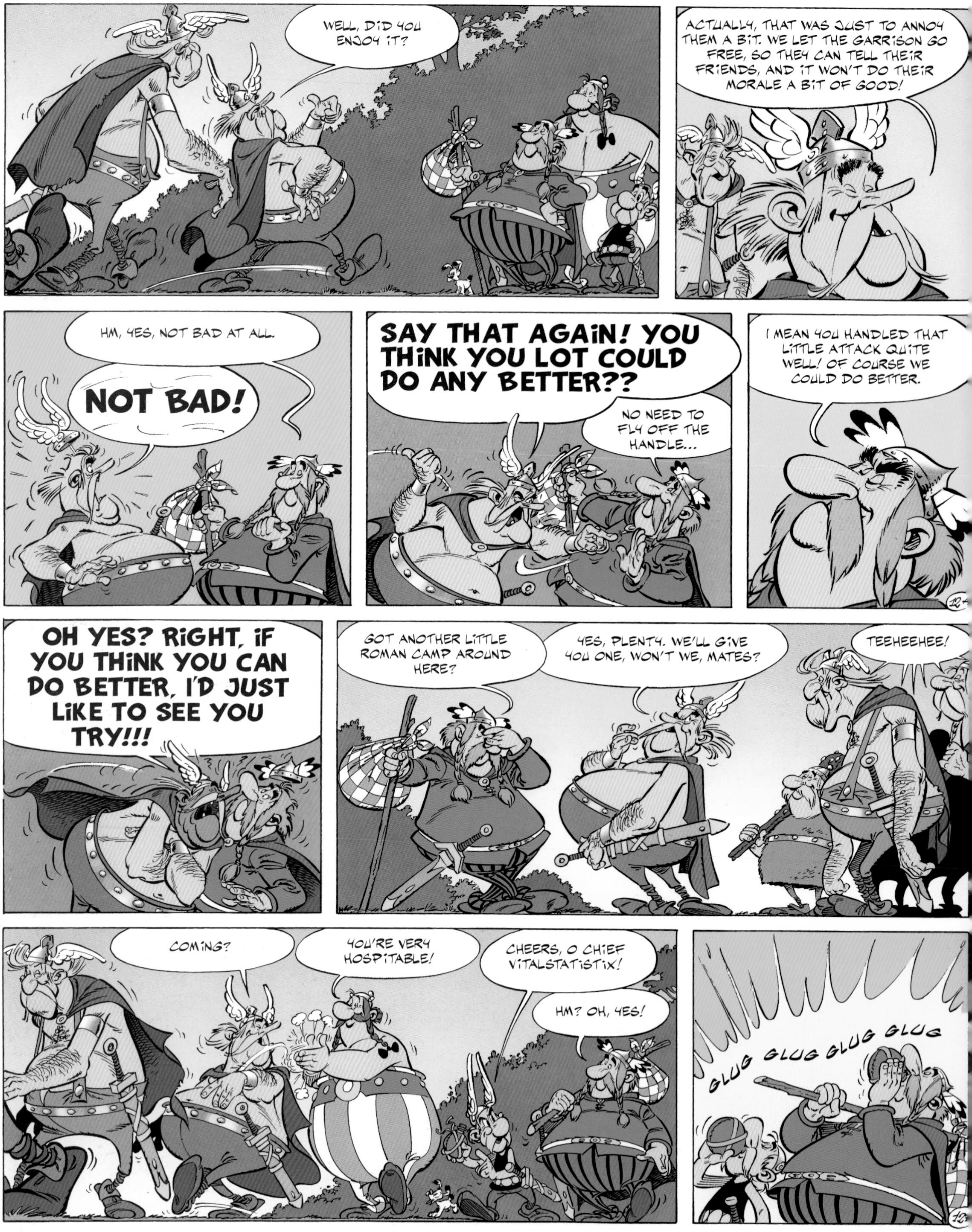
WELL, DID YOU ENJOY IT?
ACTUALLY, THAT WAS JUST TO ANNOY THEM A BIT. WE LET THE GARRISON GO FREE, SO THEY CAN TELL THEIR FRIENDS, AND IT WON'T DO THEIR MORALE A BIT OF GOOD!
HM, YES, NOT BAD AT ALL.
NOT BAD!
SAY THAT AGAIN! YOU THINK YOU LOT COULD DO ANY BETTER??
NO NEED TO FLY OFF THE HANDLE...
I MEAN YOU HANDLED THAT LITTLE ATTACK QUITE WELL! OF COURSE WE COULD DO BETTER.
OH YES? RIGHT, IF YOU THINK YOU CAN DO BETTER, I'D JUST LIKE TO SEE YOU TRY!!!
GOT ANOTHER LITTLE ROMAN CAMP AROUND HERE?
YES, PLENTY. WE'LL GIVE YOU ONE, WON'T WE, MATES?
TEEHEEHEE!
COMING?
YOU'RE VERY HOSPITABLE!
CHEERS, O CHIEF VITALSTATISTIX!
HM? OH, YES!
GLUG GLUG GLUG GLUG

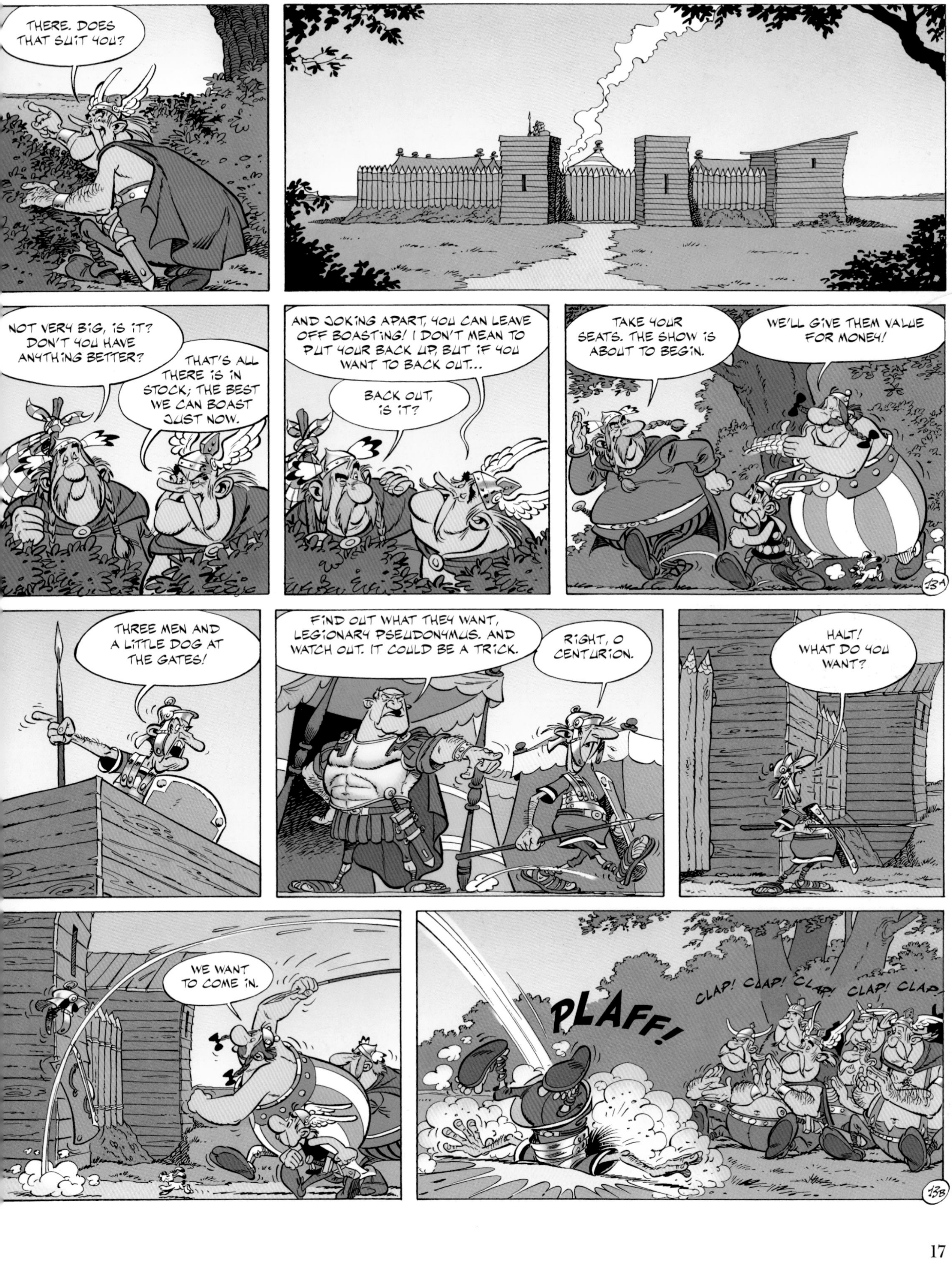
THERE. DOES THAT SUIT YOU?
NOT VERY BIG, IS IT? DON'T YOU HAVE ANYTHING BETTER?
THAT'S ALL THERE IS IN STOCK; THE BEST WE CAN BOAST JUST NOW.
AND JOKING APART, YOU CAN LEAVE OFF BOASTING! I DON'T MEAN TO PUT YOUR BACK UP, BUT IF YOU WANT TO BACK OUT...
BACK OUT, IS IT?
TAKE YOUR SEATS. THE SHOW IS ABOUT TO BEGIN.
WE'LL GIVE THEM VALUE FOR MONEY!
THREE MEN AND A LITTLE DOG AT THE GATES!
FIND OUT WHAT THEY WANT, LEGIONARY PSEUDONYMUS. AND WATCH OUT. IT COULD BE A TRICK.
RIGHT, O CENTURION.
HALT! WHAT DO YOU WANT?
WE WANT TO COME IN.
PLAFF!
CLAP! CLAP! CLAP! CLAP! CLAP!

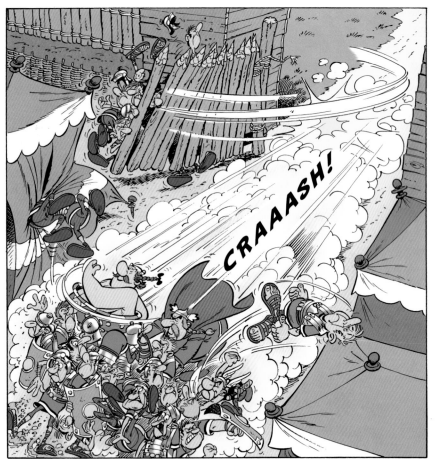

CRAAASH!

IT IS A TRICK!
IT IS A TRICK!

SLAP! SLAP! SLAP! SLAP!

I FEEL QUITE AT HOME HERE. THEIR LEGIONARIES ARE JUST LIKE OURS.

PAF!

SOON AFTERWARDS...

WELL... I THINK THAT'S OVER.

ALREADY? BUT WE'VE ONLY JUST BEGUN!

HAVE THEY GONE?

SSH! KEEP STILL.

COME ON, BOYS! I CAN'T WAIT TO SEE THE BELGIANS' FACES.

WELL, HOW DID YOU LIKE THAT, BELGIANS?

NOT BAD. QUITE AMUSING.

WHAT DO YOU MEAN, QUITE AMUSING?

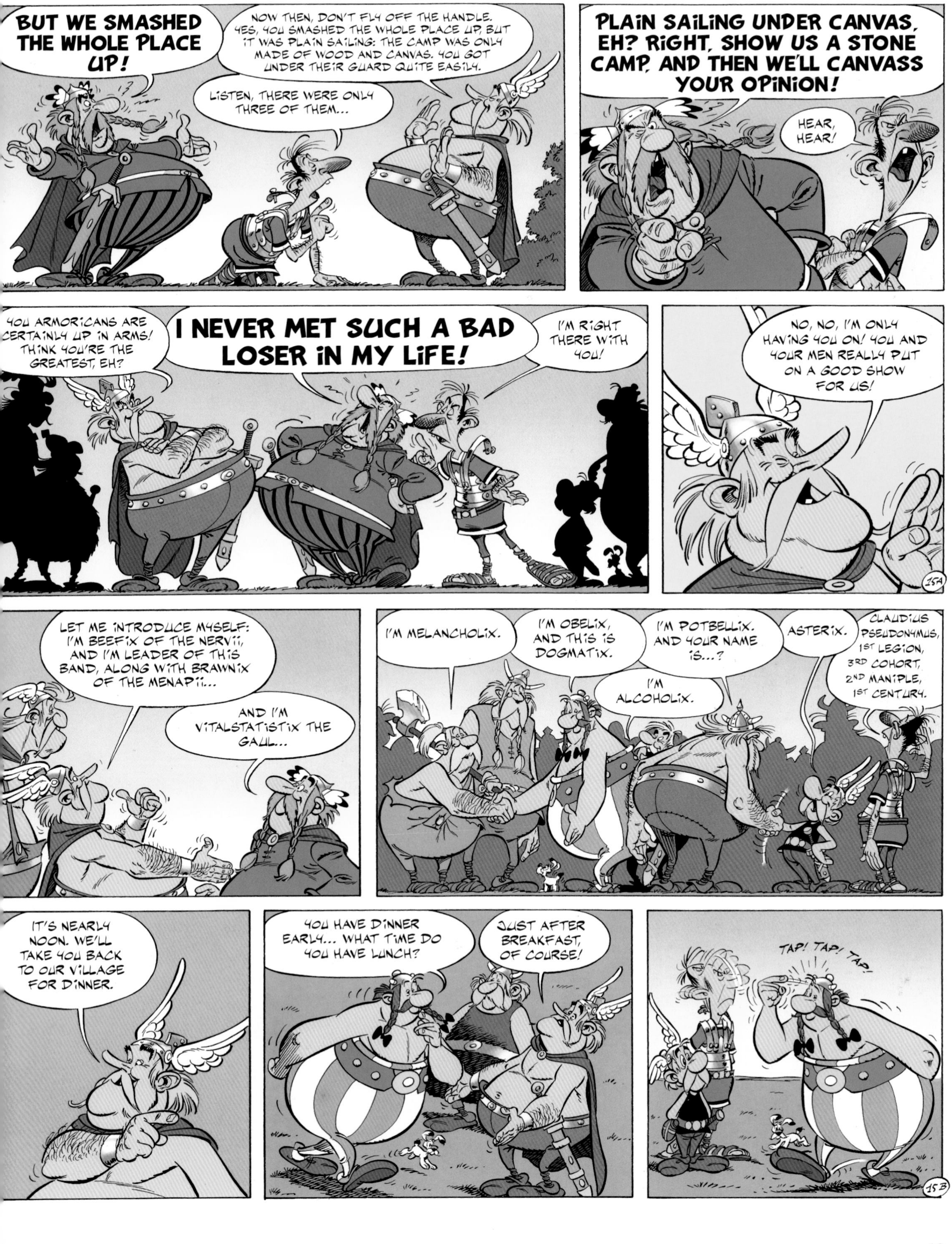
BUT WE SMASHED THE WHOLE PLACE UP!
NOW THEN, DON'T FLY OFF THE HANDLE. YES, YOU SMASHED THE WHOLE PLACE UP, BUT IT WAS PLAIN SAILING: THE CAMP WAS ONLY MADE OF WOOD AND CANVAS. YOU GOT UNDER THEIR GUARD QUITE EASILY.
LISTEN, THERE WERE ONLY THREE OF THEM...
PLAIN SAILING UNDER CANVAS, EH? RIGHT, SHOW US A STONE CAMP, AND THEN WE'LL CANVASS YOUR OPINION!
HEAR, HEAR!
YOU ARMORICANS ARE CERTAINLY UP IN ARMS! THINK YOU'RE THE GREATEST, EH?
I NEVER MET SUCH A BAD LOSER IN MY LIFE!
I'M RIGHT THERE WITH YOU!
NO, NO, I'M ONLY HAVING YOU ON! YOU AND YOUR MEN REALLY PUT ON A GOOD SHOW FOR US!
LET ME INTRODUCE MYSELF: I'M BEEFIX OF THE NERVII, AND I'M LEADER OF THIS BAND, ALONG WITH BRAWNIX OF THE MENAPII...
AND I'M VITALSTATISTIX THE GAUL...
I'M MELANCHOLIX.
I'M OBELIX, AND THIS IS DOGMATIX.
I'M POTBELLIX. AND YOUR NAME IS...?
I'M ALCOHOLIX.
ASTERIX.
CLAUDIUS PSEUDONYMUS, 1ST LEGION, 3RD COHORT, 2ND MANIPLE, 1ST CENTURY.
IT'S NEARLY NOON. WE'LL TAKE YOU BACK TO OUR VILLAGE FOR DINNER.
YOU HAVE DINNER EARLY... WHAT TIME DO YOU HAVE LUNCH?
JUST AFTER BREAKFAST, OF COURSE!
TAP! TAP! TAP!

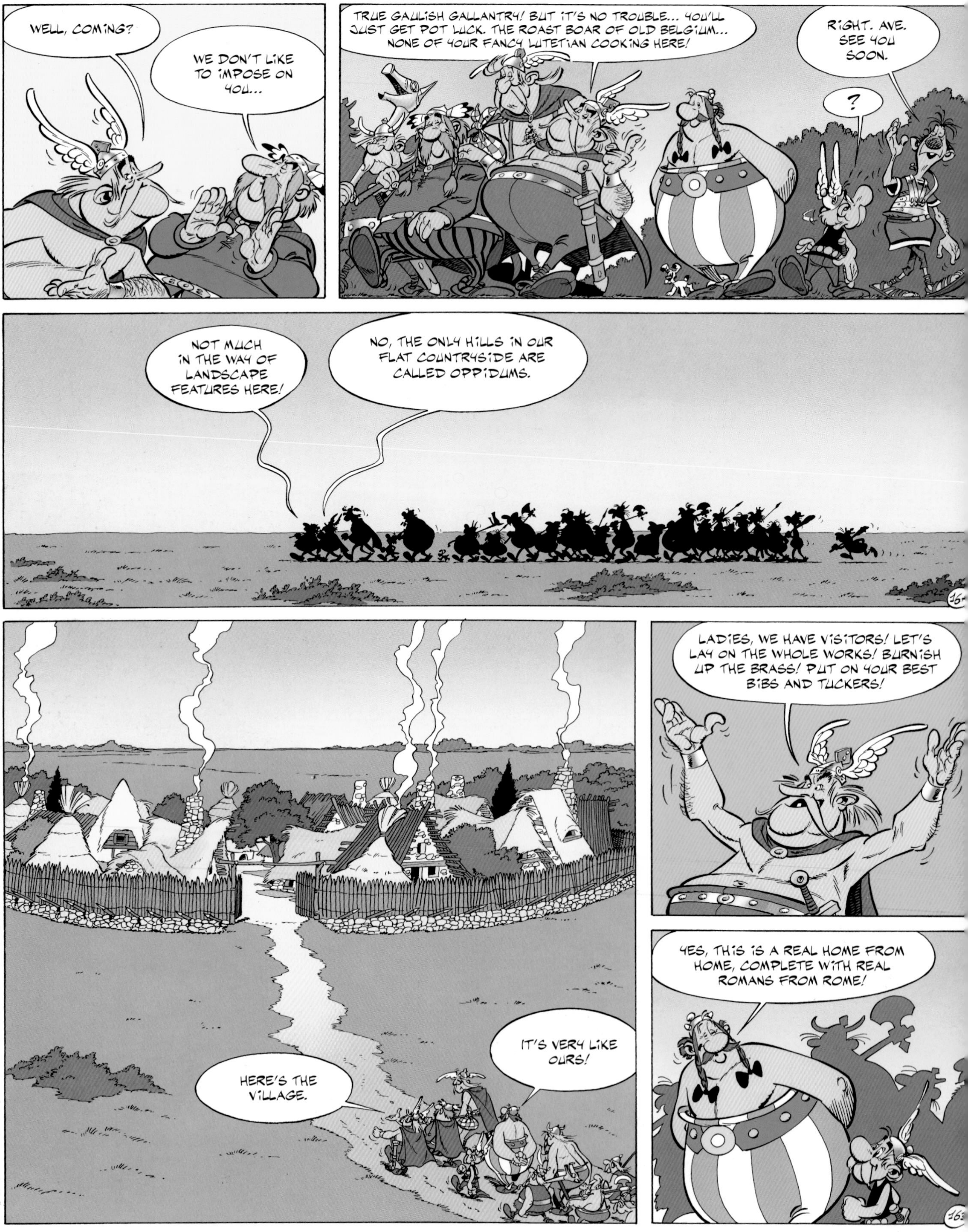

WELL, COMING?
WE DON'T LIKE TO IMPOSE ON YOU...
TRUE GAULISH GALLANTRY! BUT IT'S NO TROUBLE... YOU'LL JUST GET POT LUCK. THE ROAST BOAR OF OLD BELGIUM... NONE OF YOUR FANCY LUTETIAN COOKING HERE!
?
RIGHT. AVE. SEE YOU SOON.
NOT MUCH IN THE WAY OF LANDSCAPE FEATURES HERE!
NO, THE ONLY HILLS IN OUR FLAT COUNTRYSIDE ARE CALLED OPPIDUMS.
HERE'S THE VILLAGE.
IT'S VERY LIKE OURS!
LADIES, WE HAVE VISITORS! LET'S LAY ON THE WHOLE WORKS! BURNISH UP THE BRASS! PUT ON YOUR BEST BIBS AND TUCKERS!
YES, THIS IS A REAL HOME FROM HOME, COMPLETE WITH REAL ROMANS FROM ROME!

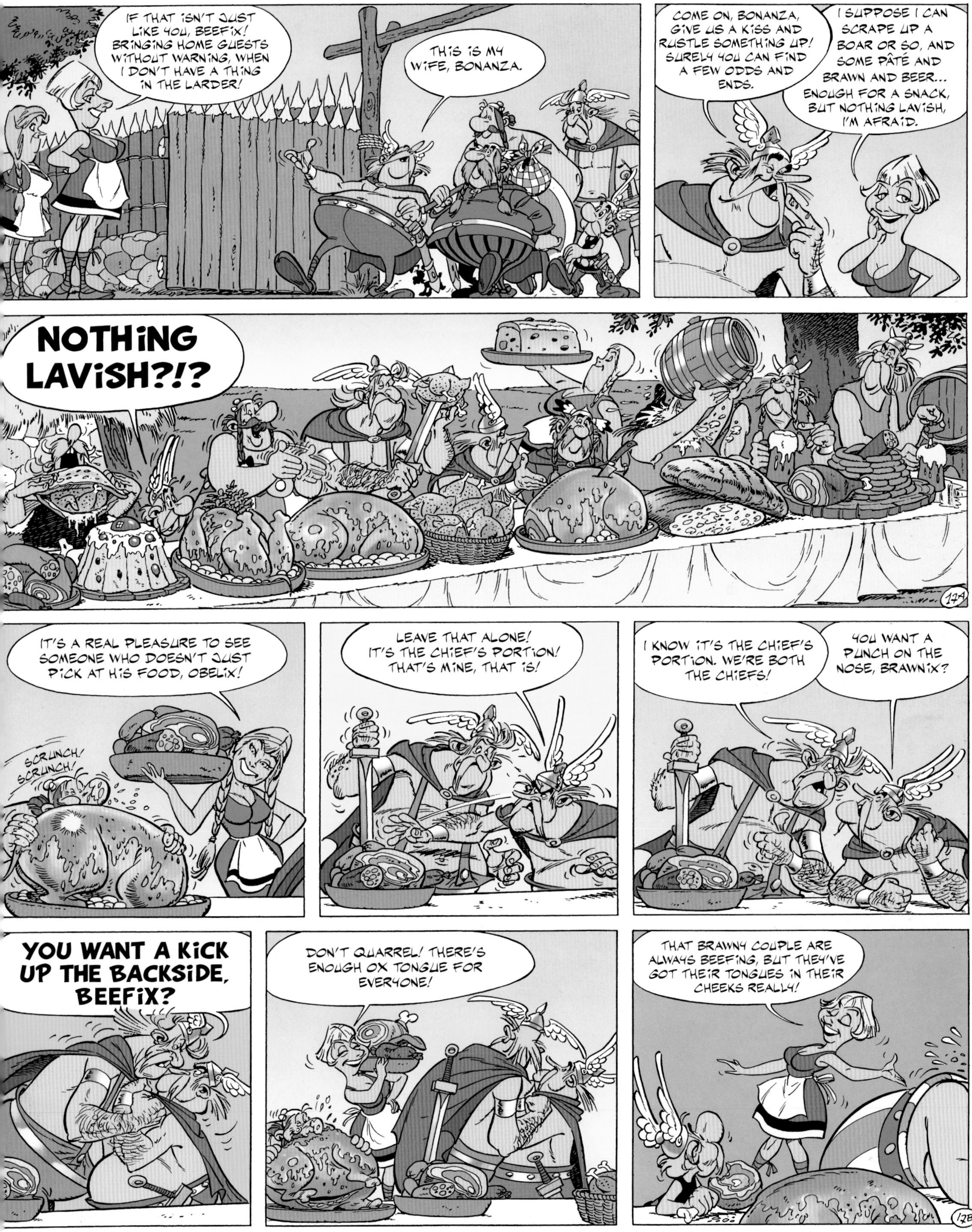
IF THAT ISN'T JUST LIKE YOU, BEEFIX! BRINGING HOME GUESTS WITHOUT WARNING, WHEN I DON'T HAVE A THING IN THE LARDER!
THIS IS MY WIFE, BONANZA.
COME ON, BONANZA, GIVE US A KISS AND RUSTLE SOMETHING UP! SURELY YOU CAN FIND A FEW ODDS AND ENDS.
I SUPPOSE I CAN SCRAPE UP A BOAR OR SO, AND SOME PÂTÉ AND BRAWN AND BEER... ENOUGH FOR A SNACK, BUT NOTHING LAVISH, I'M AFRAID.
NOTHING LAVISH?!?
17A
IT'S A REAL PLEASURE TO SEE SOMEONE WHO DOESN'T JUST PICK AT HIS FOOD, OBELIX!
SCRUNCH! SCRUNCH!
LEAVE THAT ALONE! IT'S THE CHIEF'S PORTION! THAT'S MINE, THAT IS!
I KNOW IT'S THE CHIEF'S PORTION. WE'RE BOTH THE CHIEFS!
YOU WANT A PUNCH ON THE NOSE, BRAWNIX?
YOU WANT A KICK UP THE BACKSIDE, BEEFIX?
DON'T QUARREL! THERE'S ENOUGH OX TONGUE FOR EVERYONE!
THAT BRAWNY COUPLE ARE ALWAYS BEEFING, BUT THEY'VE GOT THEIR TONGUES IN THEIR CHEEKS REALLY!
17B

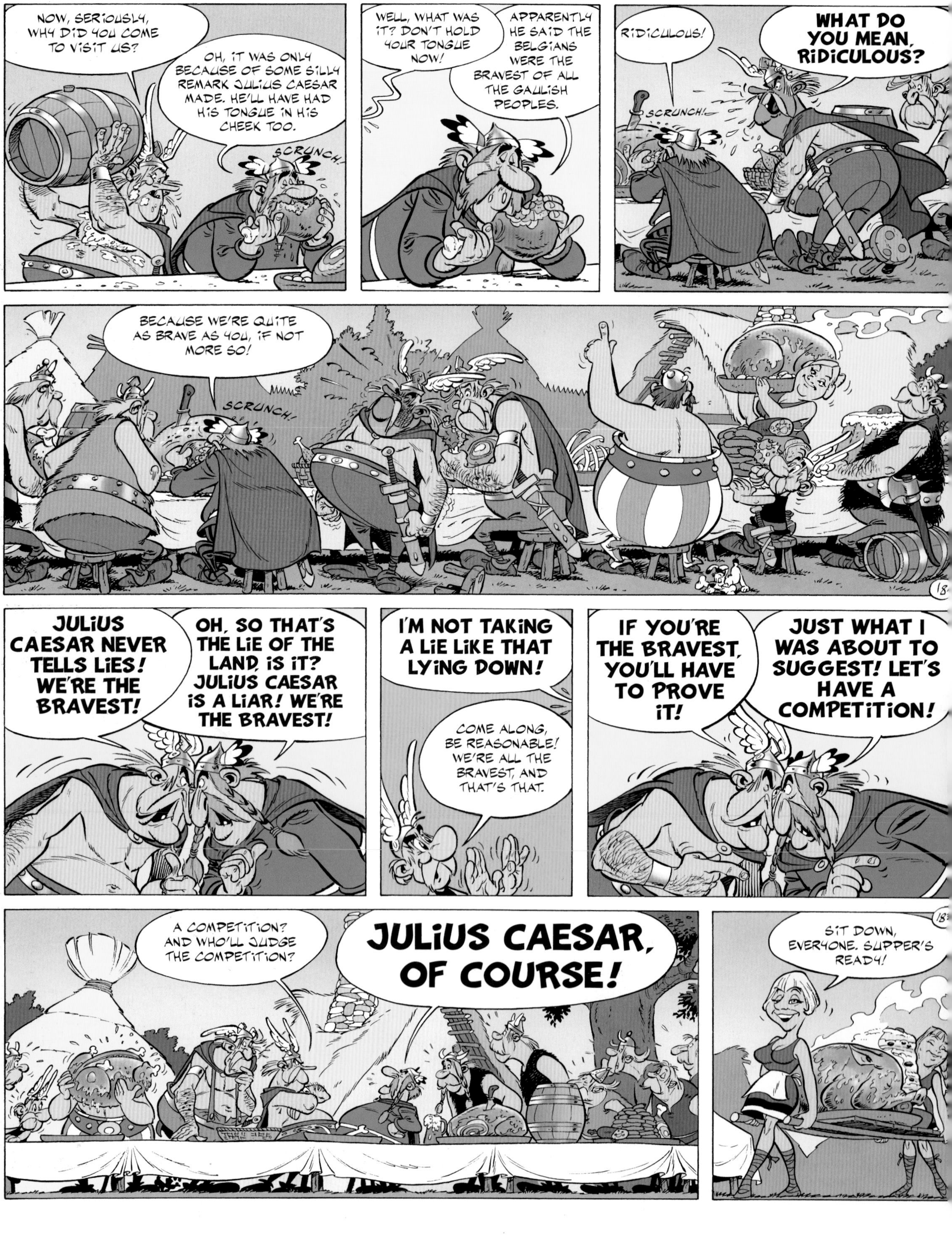
NOW, SERIOUSLY, WHY DID YOU COME TO VISIT US?
OH, IT WAS ONLY BECAUSE OF SOME SILLY REMARK JULIUS CAESAR MADE. HE'LL HAVE HAD HIS TONGUE IN HIS CHEEK TOO.
SCRUNCH!
WELL, WHAT WAS IT? DON'T HOLD YOUR TONGUE NOW!
APPARENTLY HE SAID THE BELGIANS WERE THE BRAVEST OF ALL THE GAULISH PEOPLES.
RIDICULOUS!
SCRUNCH!
WHAT DO YOU MEAN, RIDICULOUS?
BECAUSE WE'RE QUITE AS BRAVE AS YOU, IF NOT MORE SO!
SCRUNCH!
JULIUS CAESAR NEVER TELLS LIES! WE'RE THE BRAVEST!
OH, SO THAT'S THE LIE OF THE LAND, IS IT? JULIUS CAESAR IS A LIAR! WE'RE THE BRAVEST!
I'M NOT TAKING A LIE LIKE THAT LYING DOWN!
COME ALONG, BE REASONABLE! WE'RE ALL THE BRAVEST, AND THAT'S THAT.
IF YOU'RE THE BRAVEST, YOU'LL HAVE TO PROVE IT!
JUST WHAT I WAS ABOUT TO SUGGEST! LET'S HAVE A COMPETITION!
A COMPETITION? AND WHO'LL JUDGE THE COMPETITION?
JULIUS CAESAR, OF COURSE!
SIT DOWN, EVERYONE. SUPPER'S READY!

THAT NIGHT...

I DON'T LIKE THE IDEA OF THIS COMPETITION TOO MUCH. IT COULD BE A STICKY BUSINESS AFTER ALL.

I LIKE THIS COUNTRY, AND I LIKE THE PEOPLE TOO. THEY STICK AT NOTHING! LET'S GO TO SLEEP. I DON'T WANT TO BE LATE FOR BREAKFAST-AND-LUNCH.

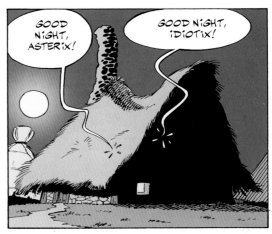

GOOD NIGHT, ASTERIX!

GOOD NIGHT, IDIOTIX!

NEXT MORNING...

COME AND GET IT!

HERE'S THE MAP SHOWING THE ROMAN CAMPS ROUND ABOUT. NOW, I SUGGEST YOU ATTACK THE CAMPS TO THE NORTH AND WE ATTACK THE CAMPS TO THE SOUTH.

SCRUNCH! SCRUNCH! SCRUNCH!

AND WE'LL SEE WHO KNOCKS DOWN THE MOST!

IF CAESAR'S GOING TO REFEREE THE MATCH, WE MUST MAKE SURE WE IDENTIFY OURSELVES TO THE ROMANS.

AND TO BE PERFECTLY HONEST, I OUGHT TO TELL YOU WE USE A MAGIC POTION. IF YOU'D CARE FOR A DROP...

NO, WE DON'T NEED ANY OF THAT! OUR BEER IS STRONG ENOUGH FOR US!

I'LL MAKE SOME SANDWICHES. YOU CAN'T GO OFF FIGHTING WITHOUT A PACKED LUNCH, DINNER AND SUPPER.

LATER, IN A ROMAN CAMP TO THE NORTH OF THE BELGIAN VILLAGE...

THERE ARE THREE MEN AND A DOG APPROACHING THE CAMP!

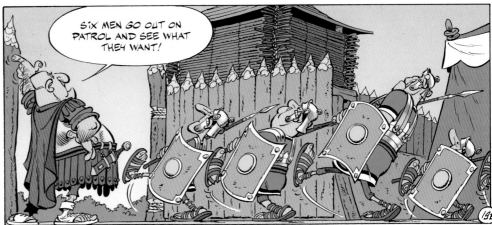

SIX MEN GO OUT ON PATROL AND SEE WHAT THEY WANT!

23

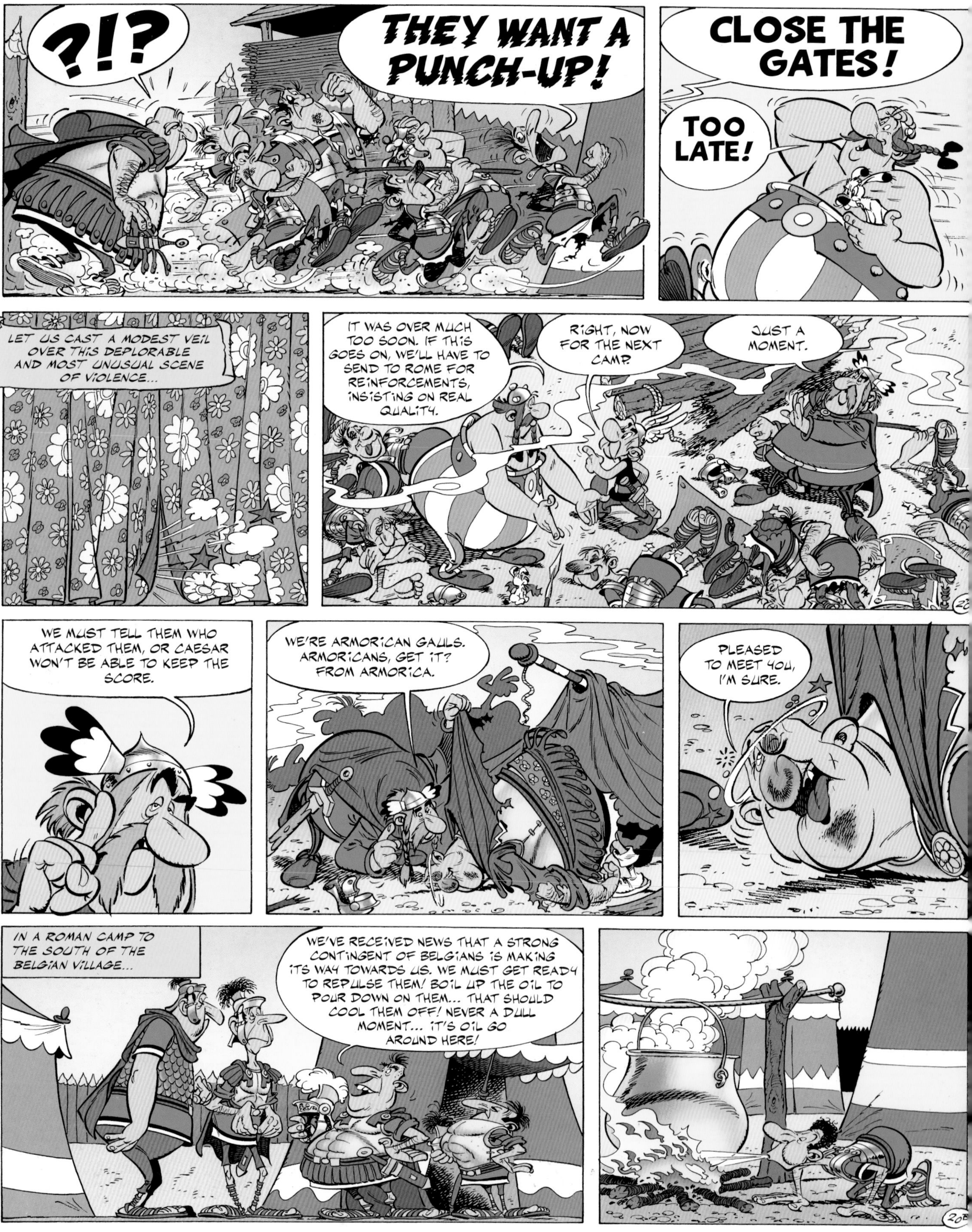
?!?
THEY WANT A PUNCH-UP!
CLOSE THE GATES!
TOO LATE!
LET US CAST A MODEST VEIL OVER THIS DEPLORABLE AND MOST UNUSUAL SCENE OF VIOLENCE...
IT WAS OVER MUCH TOO SOON. IF THIS GOES ON, WE'LL HAVE TO SEND TO ROME FOR REINFORCEMENTS, INSISTING ON REAL QUALITY.
RIGHT, NOW FOR THE NEXT CAMP?
JUST A MOMENT.
WE MUST TELL THEM WHO ATTACKED THEM, OR CAESAR WON'T BE ABLE TO KEEP THE SCORE.
WE'RE ARMORICAN GAULS. ARMORICANS, GET IT? FROM ARMORICA.
PLEASED TO MEET YOU, I'M SURE.
IN A ROMAN CAMP TO THE SOUTH OF THE BELGIAN VILLAGE...
WE'VE RECEIVED NEWS THAT A STRONG CONTINGENT OF BELGIANS IS MAKING ITS WAY TOWARDS US. WE MUST GET READY TO REPULSE THEM! BOIL UP THE OIL TO POUR DOWN ON THEM... THAT SHOULD COOL THEM OFF! NEVER A DULL MOMENT... IT'S OIL GO AROUND HERE!

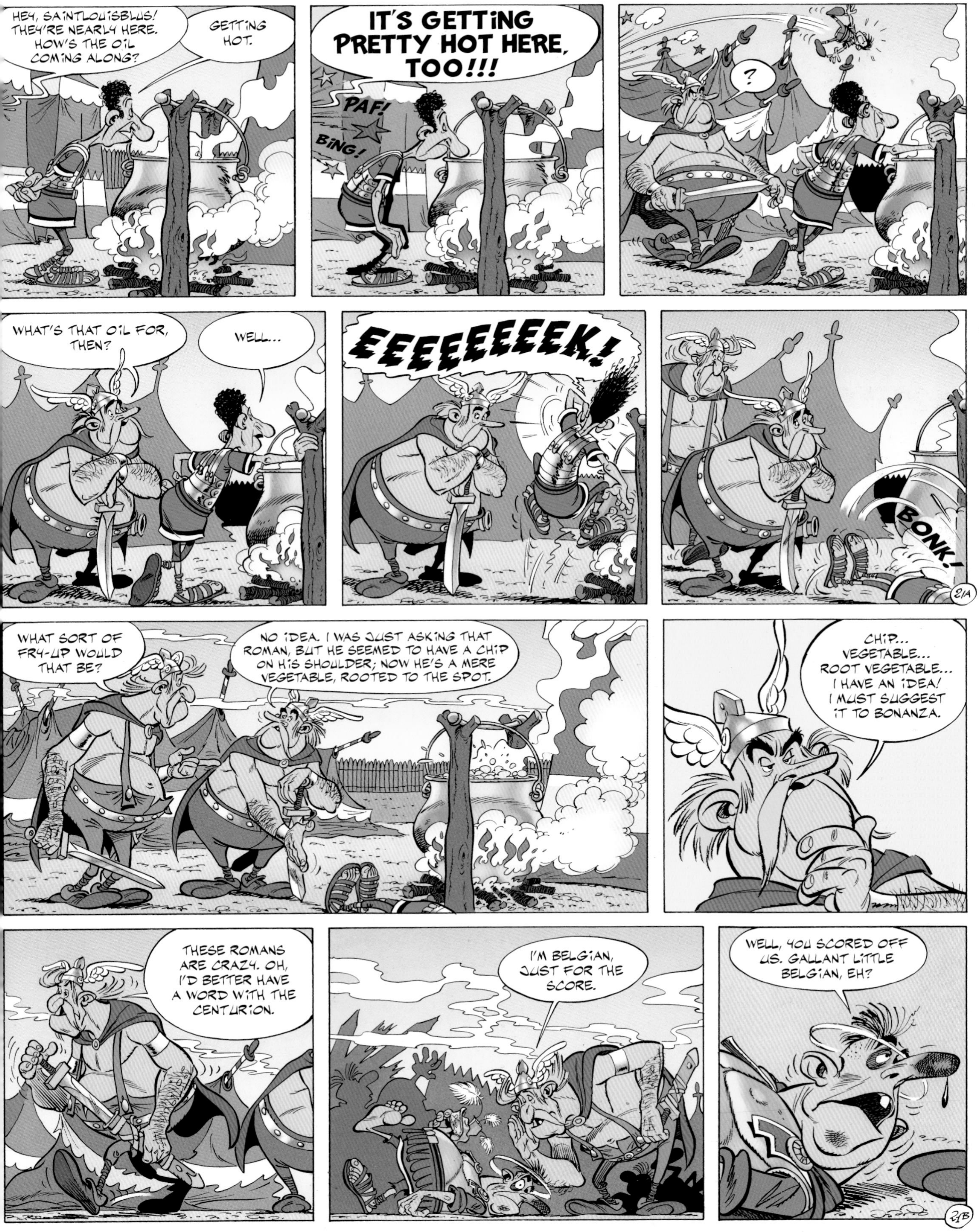
HEY, SAINTLOUISBLUS! THEY'RE NEARLY HERE. HOW'S THE OIL COMING ALONG?
GETTING HOT.
IT'S GETTING PRETTY HOT HERE, TOO!!!
PAF!
BING!
?
WHAT'S THAT OIL FOR, THEN?
WELL...
EEEEEEEEEK!
BONK!
21A
WHAT SORT OF FRY-UP WOULD THAT BE?
NO IDEA. I WAS JUST ASKING THAT ROMAN, BUT HE SEEMED TO HAVE A CHIP ON HIS SHOULDER; NOW HE'S A MERE VEGETABLE, ROOTED TO THE SPOT.
CHIP... VEGETABLE... ROOT VEGETABLE... I HAVE AN IDEA! I MUST SUGGEST IT TO BONANZA.
THESE ROMANS ARE CRAZY. OH, I'D BETTER HAVE A WORD WITH THE CENTURION.
I'M BELGIAN, JUST FOR THE SCORE.
WELL, YOU SCORED OFF US. GALLANT LITTLE BELGIAN, EH?
21B

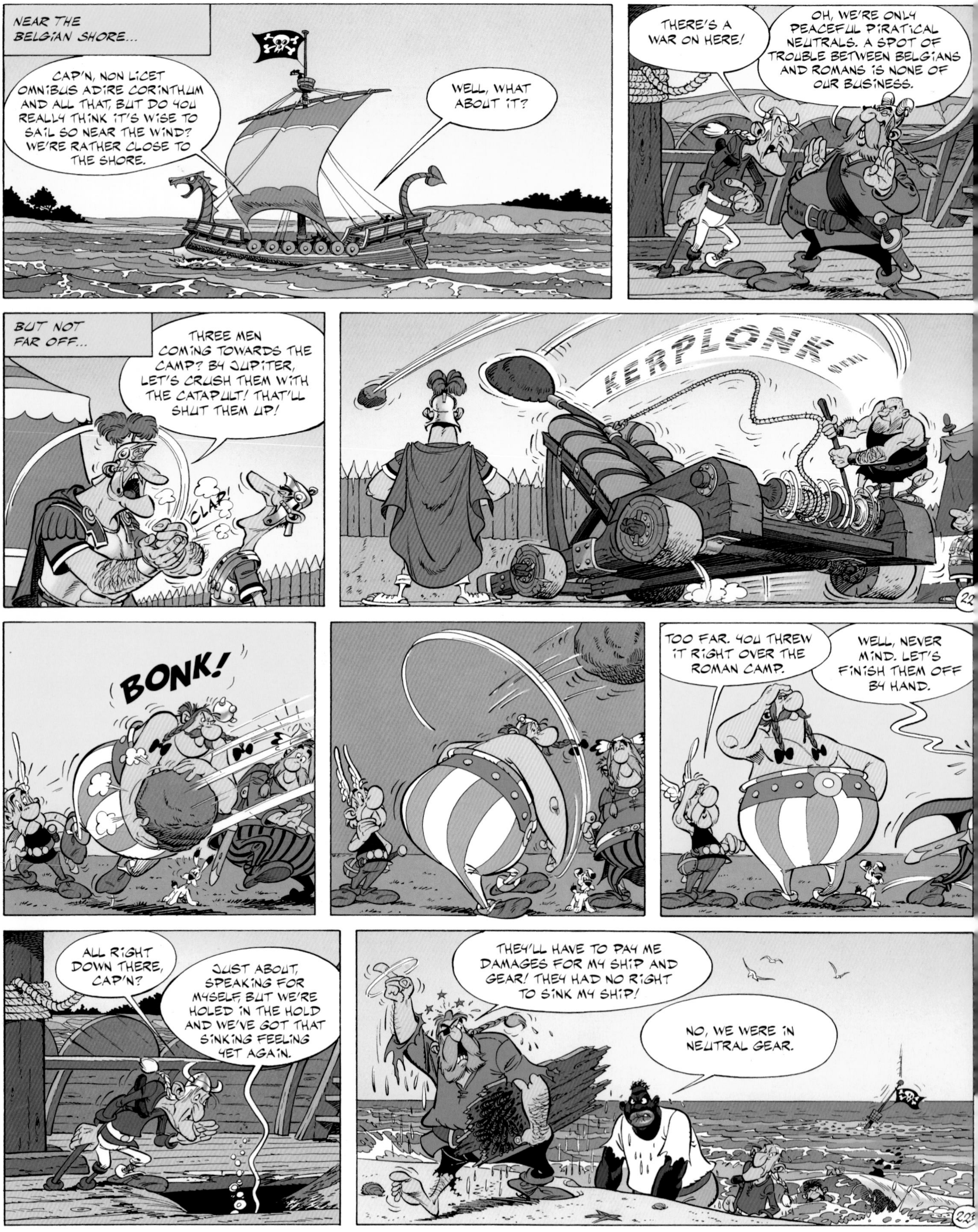

NEAR THE BELGIAN SHORE...
CAP'N, NON LICET OMNIBUS ADIRE CORINTHUM AND ALL THAT, BUT DO YOU REALLY THINK IT'S WISE TO SAIL SO NEAR THE WIND? WE'RE RATHER CLOSE TO THE SHORE.
WELL, WHAT ABOUT IT?
THERE'S A WAR ON HERE!
OH, WE'RE ONLY PEACEFUL PIRATICAL NEUTRALS. A SPOT OF TROUBLE BETWEEN BELGIANS AND ROMANS IS NONE OF OUR BUSINESS.
BUT NOT FAR OFF...
THREE MEN COMING TOWARDS THE CAMP? BY JUPITER, LET'S CRUSH THEM WITH THE CATAPULT! THAT'LL SHUT THEM UP!
CLAP!
KERPLONK!
BONK!
TOO FAR. YOU THREW IT RIGHT OVER THE ROMAN CAMP.
WELL, NEVER MIND. LET'S FINISH THEM OFF BY HAND.
ALL RIGHT DOWN THERE, CAP'N?
JUST ABOUT, SPEAKING FOR MYSELF, BUT WE'RE HOLED IN THE HOLD AND WE'VE GOT THAT SINKING FEELING YET AGAIN.
THEY'LL HAVE TO PAY ME DAMAGES FOR MY SHIP AND GEAR! THEY HAD NO RIGHT TO SINK MY SHIP!
NO, WE WERE IN NEUTRAL GEAR.

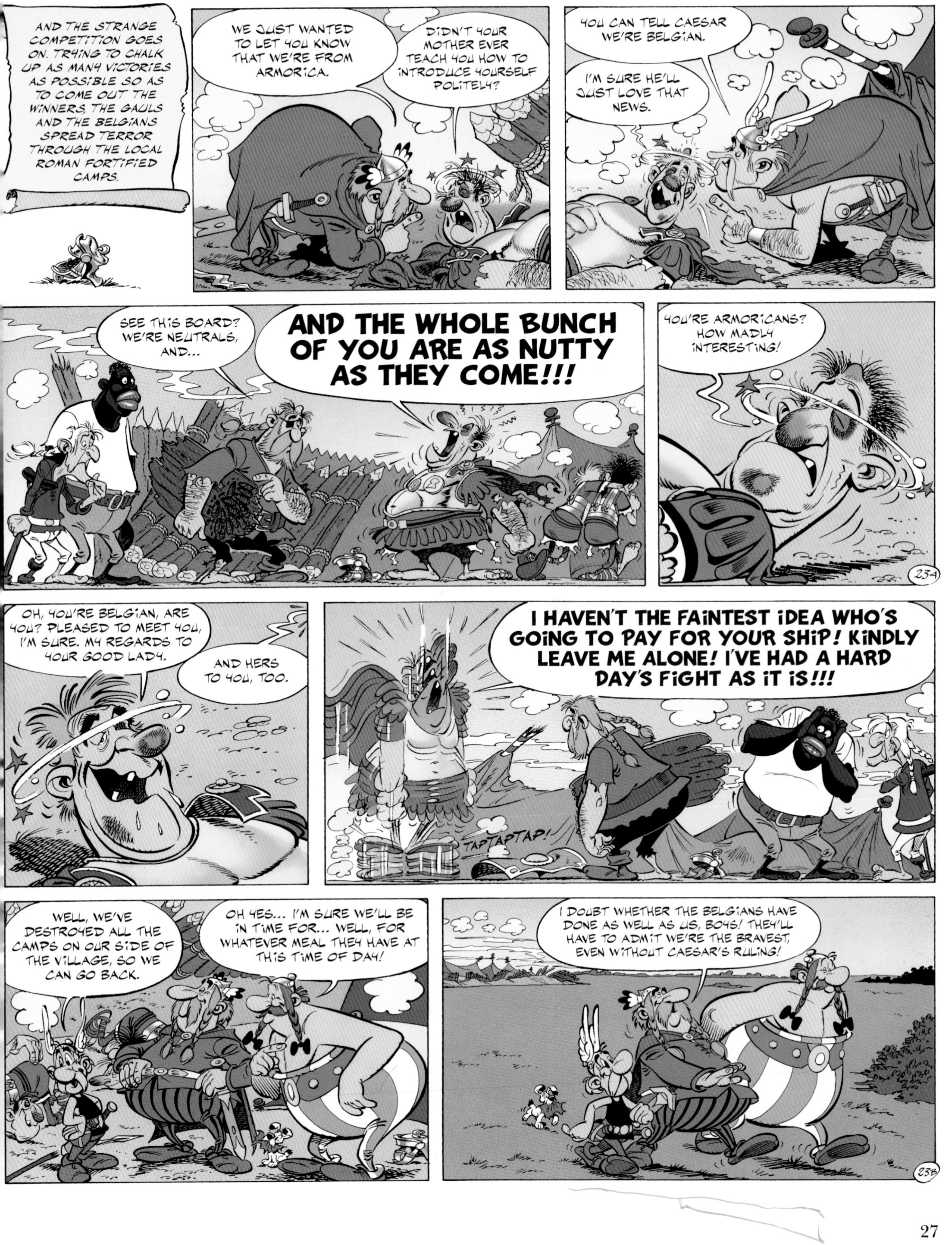

AND THE STRANGE COMPETITION GOES ON. TRYING TO CHALK UP AS MANY VICTORIES AS POSSIBLE SO AS TO COME OUT THE WINNERS, THE GAULS AND THE BELGIANS SPREAD TERROR THROUGH THE LOCAL ROMAN FORTIFIED CAMPS.
WE JUST WANTED TO LET YOU KNOW THAT WE'RE FROM ARMORICA.
DIDN'T YOUR MOTHER EVER TEACH YOU HOW TO INTRODUCE YOURSELF POLITELY?
YOU CAN TELL CAESAR WE'RE BELGIAN.
I'M SURE HE'LL JUST LOVE THAT NEWS.
SEE THIS BOARD? WE'RE NEUTRALS, AND...
AND THE WHOLE BUNCH OF YOU ARE AS NUTTY AS THEY COME!!!
YOU'RE ARMORICANS? HOW MADLY INTERESTING!
OH, YOU'RE BELGIAN, ARE YOU? PLEASED TO MEET YOU, I'M SURE. MY REGARDS TO YOUR GOOD LADY.
AND HERS TO YOU, TOO.
I HAVEN'T THE FAINTEST IDEA WHO'S GOING TO PAY FOR YOUR SHIP! KINDLY LEAVE ME ALONE! I'VE HAD A HARD DAY'S FIGHT AS IT IS!!!
TAPTAPTAP!
WELL, WE'VE DESTROYED ALL THE CAMPS ON OUR SIDE OF THE VILLAGE, SO WE CAN GO BACK.
OH YES... I'M SURE WE'LL BE IN TIME FOR... WELL, FOR WHATEVER MEAL THEY HAVE AT THIS TIME OF DAY!
I DOUBT WHETHER THE BELGIANS HAVE DONE AS WELL AS US, BOYS! THEY'LL HAVE TO ADMIT WE'RE THE BRAVEST, EVEN WITHOUT CAESAR'S RULING!

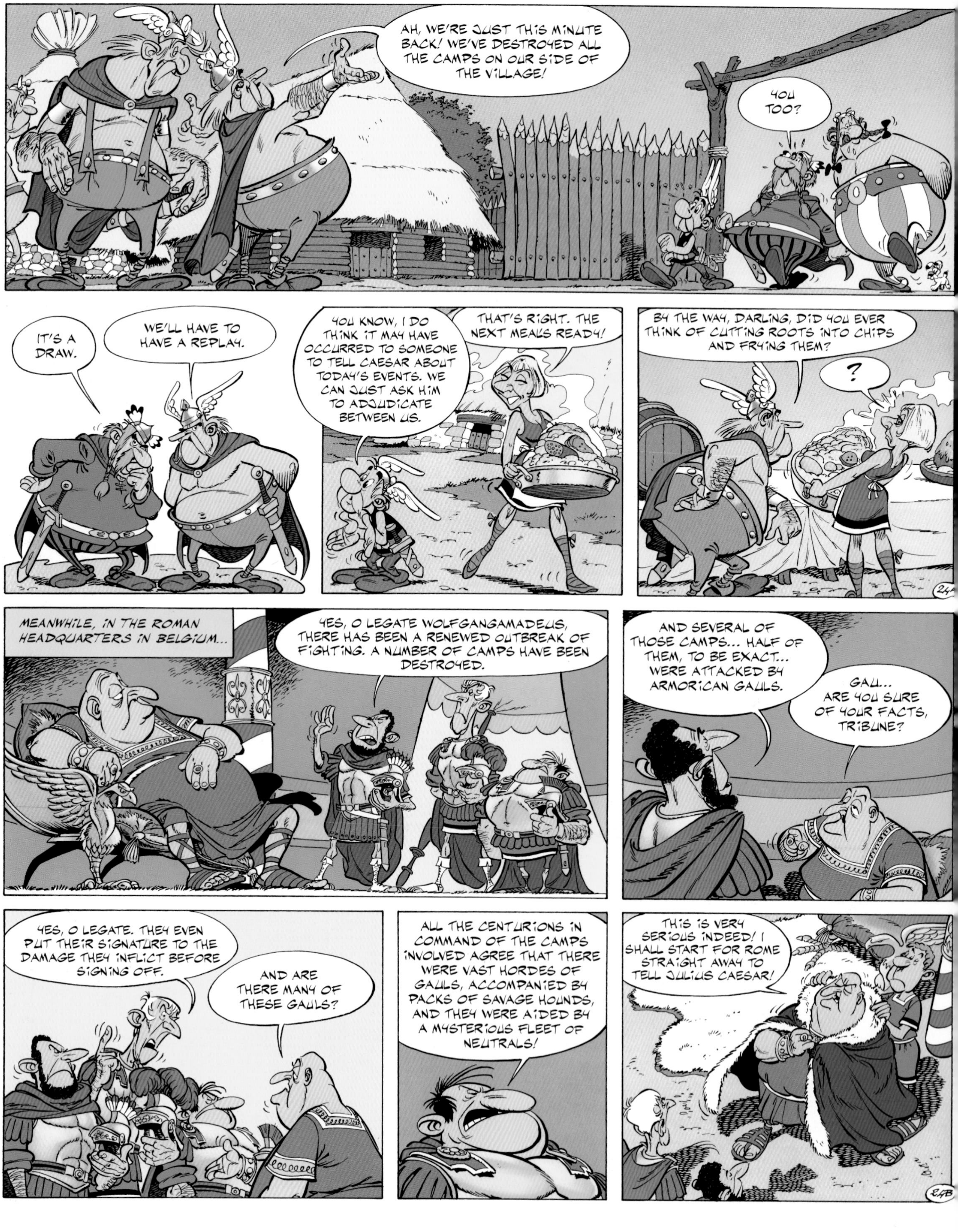
AH, WE'RE JUST THIS MINUTE BACK! WE'VE DESTROYED ALL THE CAMPS ON OUR SIDE OF THE VILLAGE!
YOU TOO?
IT'S A DRAW.
WE'LL HAVE TO HAVE A REPLAY.
YOU KNOW, I DO THINK IT MAY HAVE OCCURRED TO SOMEONE TO TELL CAESAR ABOUT TODAY'S EVENTS. WE CAN JUST ASK HIM TO ADJUDICATE BETWEEN US.
THAT'S RIGHT. THE NEXT MEAL'S READY!
BY THE WAY, DARLING, DID YOU EVER THINK OF CUTTING ROOTS INTO CHIPS AND FRYING THEM?
?
MEANWHILE, IN THE ROMAN HEADQUARTERS IN BELGIUM...
YES, O LEGATE WOLFGANGAMADEUS, THERE HAS BEEN A RENEWED OUTBREAK OF FIGHTING. A NUMBER OF CAMPS HAVE BEEN DESTROYED.
AND SEVERAL OF THOSE CAMPS... HALF OF THEM, TO BE EXACT... WERE ATTACKED BY ARMORICAN GAULS.
GAU... ARE YOU SURE OF YOUR FACTS, TRIBUNE?
YES, O LEGATE. THEY EVEN PUT THEIR SIGNATURE TO THE DAMAGE THEY INFLICT BEFORE SIGNING OFF.
AND ARE THERE MANY OF THESE GAULS?
ALL THE CENTURIONS IN COMMAND OF THE CAMPS INVOLVED AGREE THAT THERE WERE VAST HORDES OF GAULS, ACCOMPANIED BY PACKS OF SAVAGE HOUNDS, AND THEY WERE AIDED BY A MYSTERIOUS FLEET OF NEUTRALS!
THIS IS VERY SERIOUS INDEED! I SHALL START FOR ROME STRAIGHT AWAY TO TELL JULIUS CAESAR!

IN ROME, THE SENATE IS SITTING.

SENATOR MONOTONUS MAY SPEAK.

FRIENDS, ROMANS, COUNTRYMEN, OWING TO THE PERSISTENT DROUGHT THE BRASSICA OLERACEA CAPITATA* GROWERS OF THE PISAE ARE IN TROUBLE...

* CABBAGE

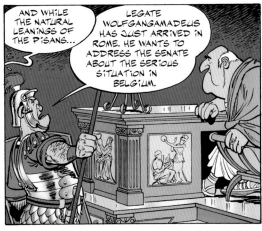

AND WHILE THE NATURAL LEANINGS OF THE PISANS...

LEGATE WOLFGANGAMADEUS HAS JUST ARRIVED IN ROME. HE WANTS TO ADDRESS THE SENATE ABOUT THE SERIOUS SITUATION IN BELGIUM.

SHOW HIM IN!

OH NO, YOU DON'T! THE RULES FORBID ANYONE TO INTERRUPT THE SPEAKER... AS I WAS SAYING, THE NATURAL LEANINGS OF THE BRASSICA GROWERS...

YES, SHOW HIM IN, DO! JULIUS CAESAR IS BLEEDING ROME WHITE WITH HIS CAMPAIGNS. I'D BE INTERESTED TO KNOW WHERE ALL THAT MONEY GOES!

...ARE TOWARDS THE CULTIVATION OF BRASSICA OLERACEA...

I AM NOT AFRAID TO HEAR LEGATE WOLFGANGAMADEUS SPEAK IN PUBLIC! LET HIM IN!

OH, STUFF YOUR BRASSICA OLERACEA CAPITATA!

BUT THE BRASSICA OLERACEA CAPITATA...

DELETE THAT LAST CULINARY EXPLETIVE OF CAESAR'S. IT WOULDN'T GO DOWN TOO WELL AS A CLASSICAL QUOTATION.

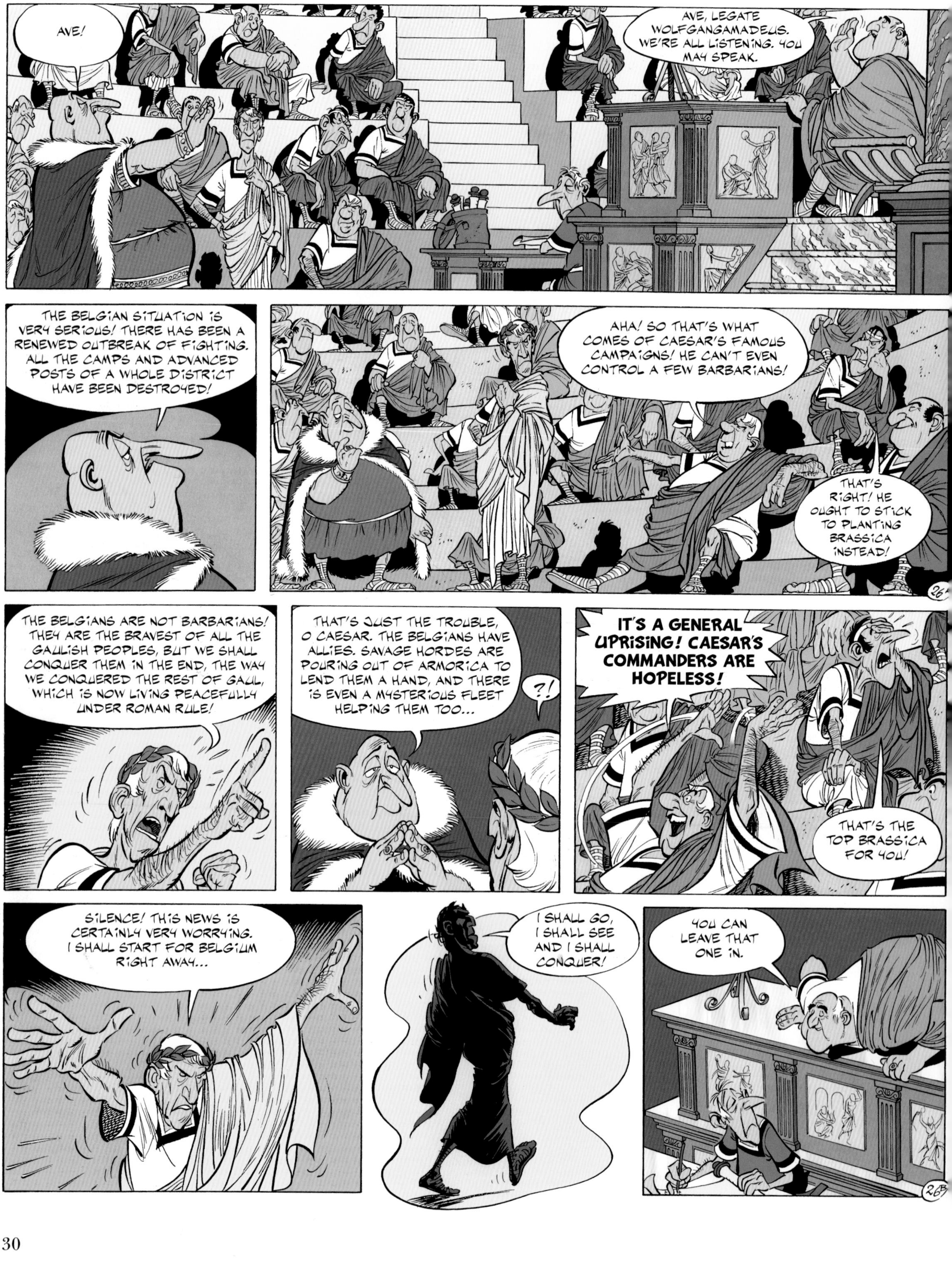
AVE!
AVE, LEGATE WOLFGANGAMADEUS. WE'RE ALL LISTENING. YOU MAY SPEAK.
THE BELGIAN SITUATION IS VERY SERIOUS! THERE HAS BEEN A RENEWED OUTBREAK OF FIGHTING. ALL THE CAMPS AND ADVANCED POSTS OF A WHOLE DISTRICT HAVE BEEN DESTROYED!
AHA! SO THAT'S WHAT COMES OF CAESAR'S FAMOUS CAMPAIGNS! HE CAN'T EVEN CONTROL A FEW BARBARIANS!
THAT'S RIGHT! HE OUGHT TO STICK TO PLANTING BRASSICA INSTEAD!
26
THE BELGIANS ARE NOT BARBARIANS! THEY ARE THE BRAVEST OF ALL THE GAULISH PEOPLES, BUT WE SHALL CONQUER THEM IN THE END, THE WAY WE CONQUERED THE REST OF GAUL, WHICH IS NOW LIVING PEACEFULLY UNDER ROMAN RULE!
THAT'S JUST THE TROUBLE, O CAESAR. THE BELGIANS HAVE ALLIES. SAVAGE HORDES ARE POURING OUT OF ARMORICA TO LEND THEM A HAND, AND THERE IS EVEN A MYSTERIOUS FLEET HELPING THEM TOO...
?!
IT'S A GENERAL UPRISING! CAESAR'S COMMANDERS ARE HOPELESS!
THAT'S THE TOP BRASSICA FOR YOU!
SILENCE! THIS NEWS IS CERTAINLY VERY WORRYING. I SHALL START FOR BELGIUM RIGHT AWAY...
I SHALL GO, I SHALL SEE AND I SHALL CONQUER!
YOU CAN LEAVE THAT ONE IN.
26B

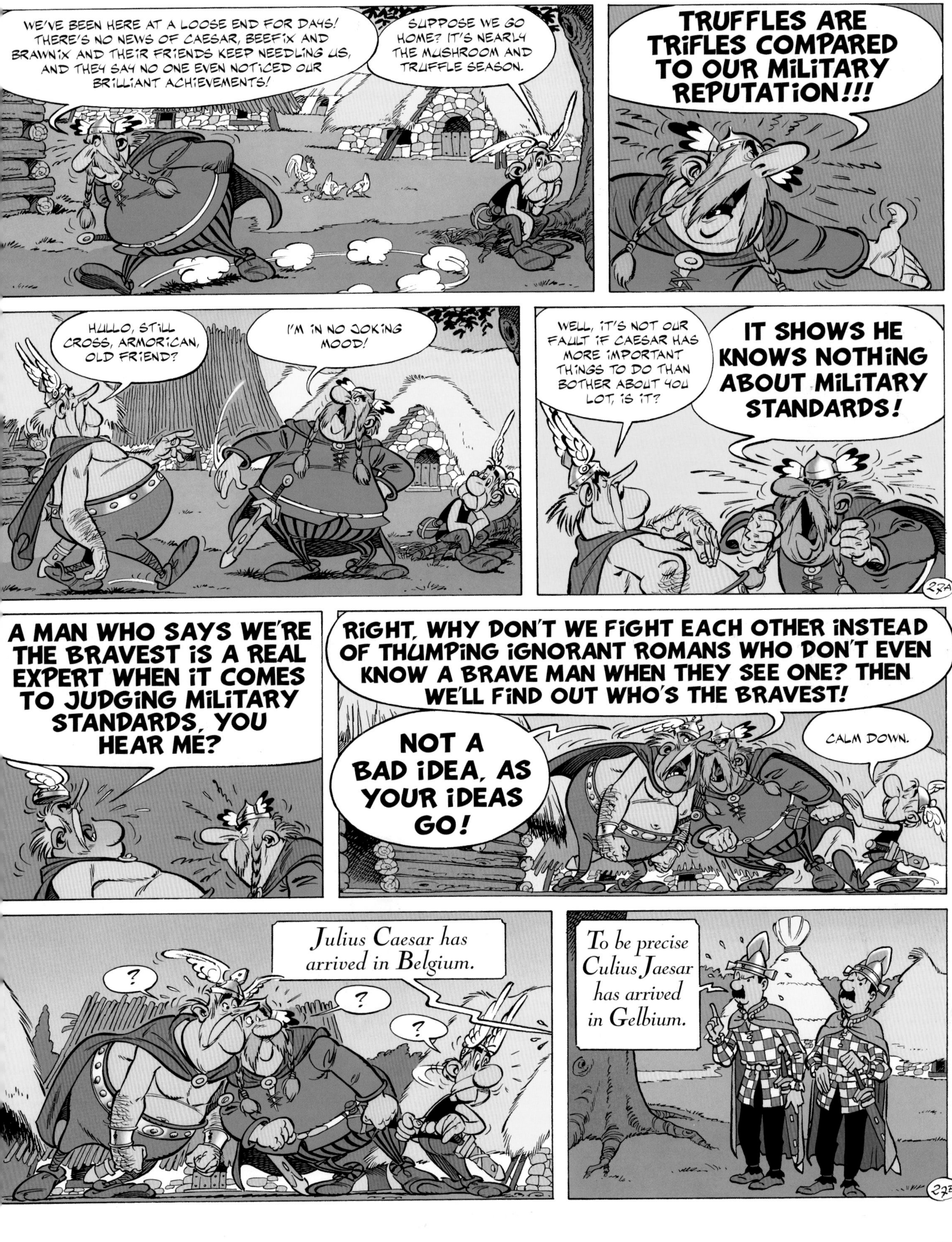

WE'VE BEEN HERE AT A LOOSE END FOR DAYS! THERE'S NO NEWS OF CAESAR, BEEFIX AND BRAWNIX AND THEIR FRIENDS KEEP NEEDLING US, AND THEY SAY NO ONE EVEN NOTICED OUR BRILLIANT ACHIEVEMENTS!
SUPPOSE WE GO HOME? IT'S NEARLY THE MUSHROOM AND TRUFFLE SEASON.
TRUFFLES ARE TRIFLES COMPARED TO OUR MILITARY REPUTATION!!!
HULLO, STILL CROSS, ARMORICAN, OLD FRIEND?
I'M IN NO JOKING MOOD!
WELL, IT'S NOT OUR FAULT IF CAESAR HAS MORE IMPORTANT THINGS TO DO THAN BOTHER ABOUT YOU LOT, IS IT?
IT SHOWS HE KNOWS NOTHING ABOUT MILITARY STANDARDS!
27A
A MAN WHO SAYS WE'RE THE BRAVEST IS A REAL EXPERT WHEN IT COMES TO JUDGING MILITARY STANDARDS, YOU HEAR ME?
RIGHT, WHY DON'T WE FIGHT EACH OTHER INSTEAD OF THUMPING IGNORANT ROMANS WHO DON'T EVEN KNOW A BRAVE MAN WHEN THEY SEE ONE? THEN WE'LL FIND OUT WHO'S THE BRAVEST!
NOT A BAD IDEA, AS YOUR IDEAS GO!
CALM DOWN.
?
Julius Caesar has arrived in Belgium.
?
?
To be precise Culius Jaesar has arrived in Gelbium.
27B

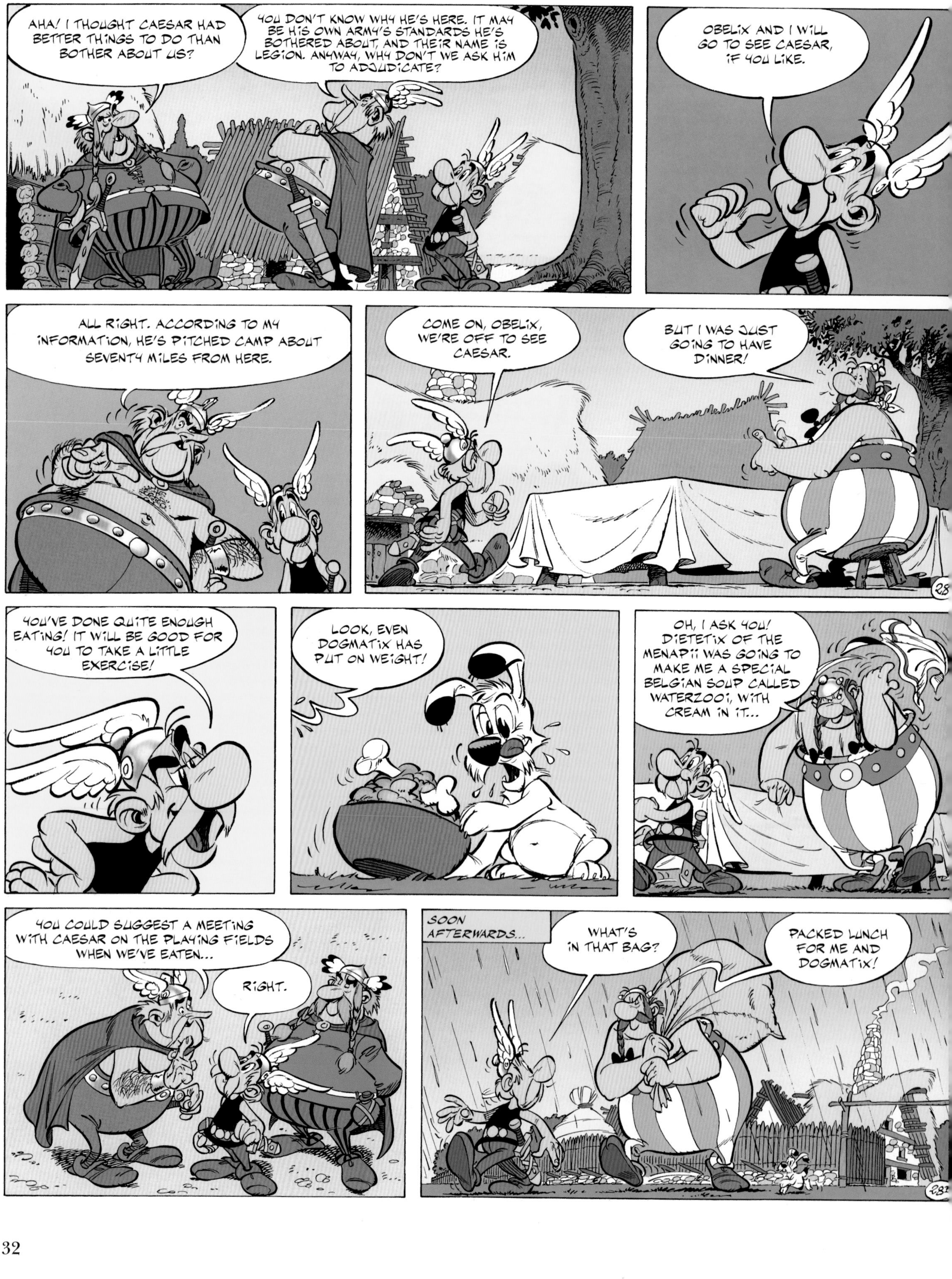
AHA! I THOUGHT CAESAR HAD BETTER THINGS TO DO THAN BOTHER ABOUT US?
YOU DON'T KNOW WHY HE'S HERE. IT MAY BE HIS OWN ARMY'S STANDARDS HE'S BOTHERED ABOUT, AND THEIR NAME IS LEGION. ANYWAY, WHY DON'T WE ASK HIM TO ADJUDICATE?
OBELIX AND I WILL GO TO SEE CAESAR, IF YOU LIKE.
ALL RIGHT. ACCORDING TO MY INFORMATION, HE'S PITCHED CAMP ABOUT SEVENTY MILES FROM HERE.
COME ON, OBELIX, WE'RE OFF TO SEE CAESAR.
BUT I WAS JUST GOING TO HAVE DINNER!
YOU'VE DONE QUITE ENOUGH EATING! IT WILL BE GOOD FOR YOU TO TAKE A LITTLE EXERCISE!
LOOK, EVEN DOGMATIX HAS PUT ON WEIGHT!
OH, I ASK YOU! DIETETIX OF THE MENAPII WAS GOING TO MAKE ME A SPECIAL BELGIAN SOUP CALLED WATERZOOI, WITH CREAM IN IT...
YOU COULD SUGGEST A MEETING WITH CAESAR ON THE PLAYING FIELDS WHEN WE'VE EATEN...
RIGHT.
SOON AFTERWARDS...
WHAT'S IN THAT BAG?
PACKED LUNCH FOR ME AND DOGMATIX!

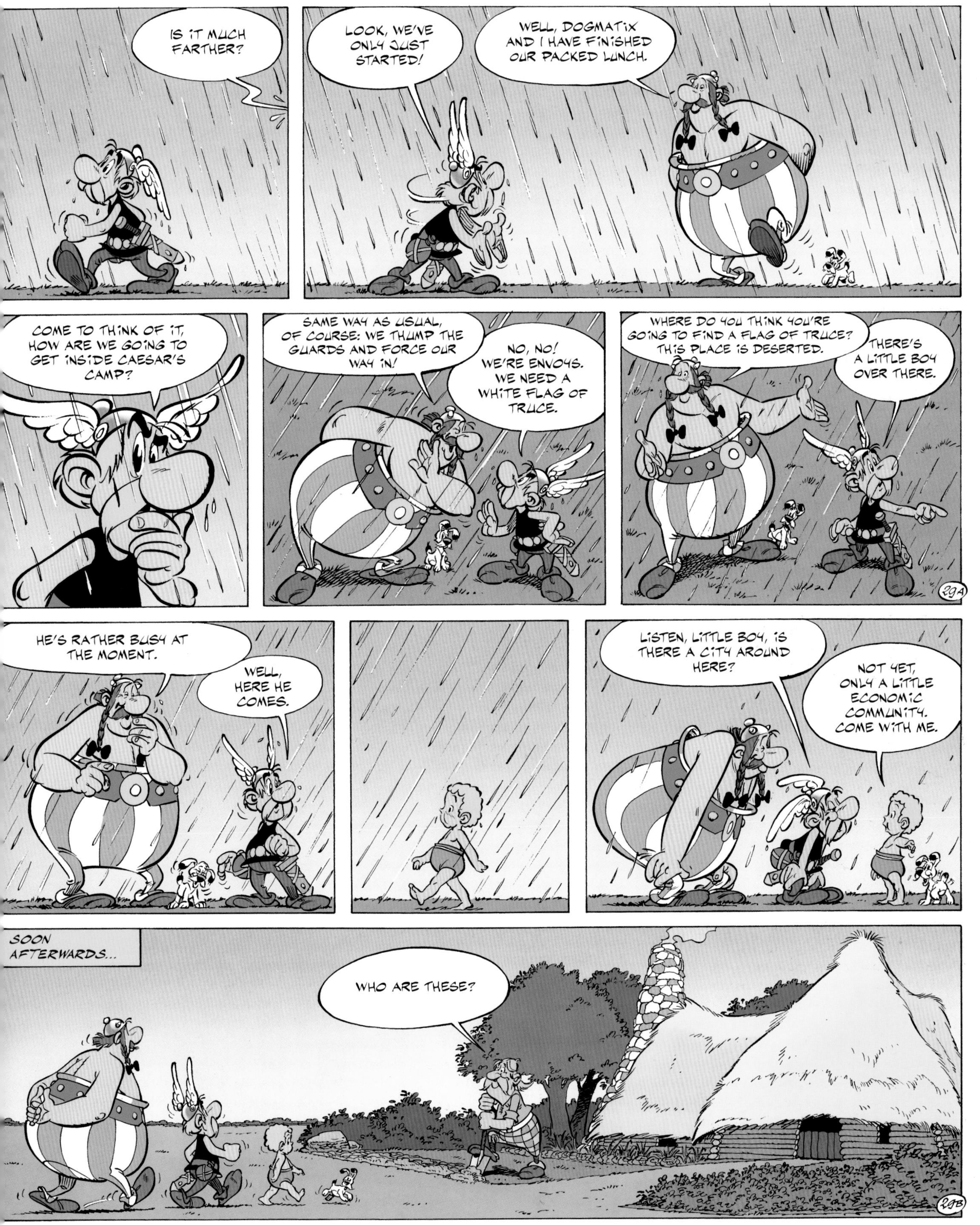
IS IT MUCH FARTHER?
LOOK, WE'VE ONLY JUST STARTED!
WELL, DOGMATIX AND I HAVE FINISHED OUR PACKED LUNCH.
COME TO THINK OF IT, HOW ARE WE GOING TO GET INSIDE CAESAR'S CAMP?
SAME WAY AS USUAL, OF COURSE: WE THUMP THE GUARDS AND FORCE OUR WAY IN!
NO, NO! WE'RE ENVOYS. WE NEED A WHITE FLAG OF TRUCE.
WHERE DO YOU THINK YOU'RE GOING TO FIND A FLAG OF TRUCE? THIS PLACE IS DESERTED.
THERE'S A LITTLE BOY OVER THERE.
HE'S RATHER BUSY AT THE MOMENT.
WELL, HERE HE COMES.
LISTEN, LITTLE BOY, IS THERE A CITY AROUND HERE?
NOT YET, ONLY A LITTLE ECONOMIC COMMUNITY. COME WITH ME.
SOON AFTERWARDS...
WHO ARE THESE?

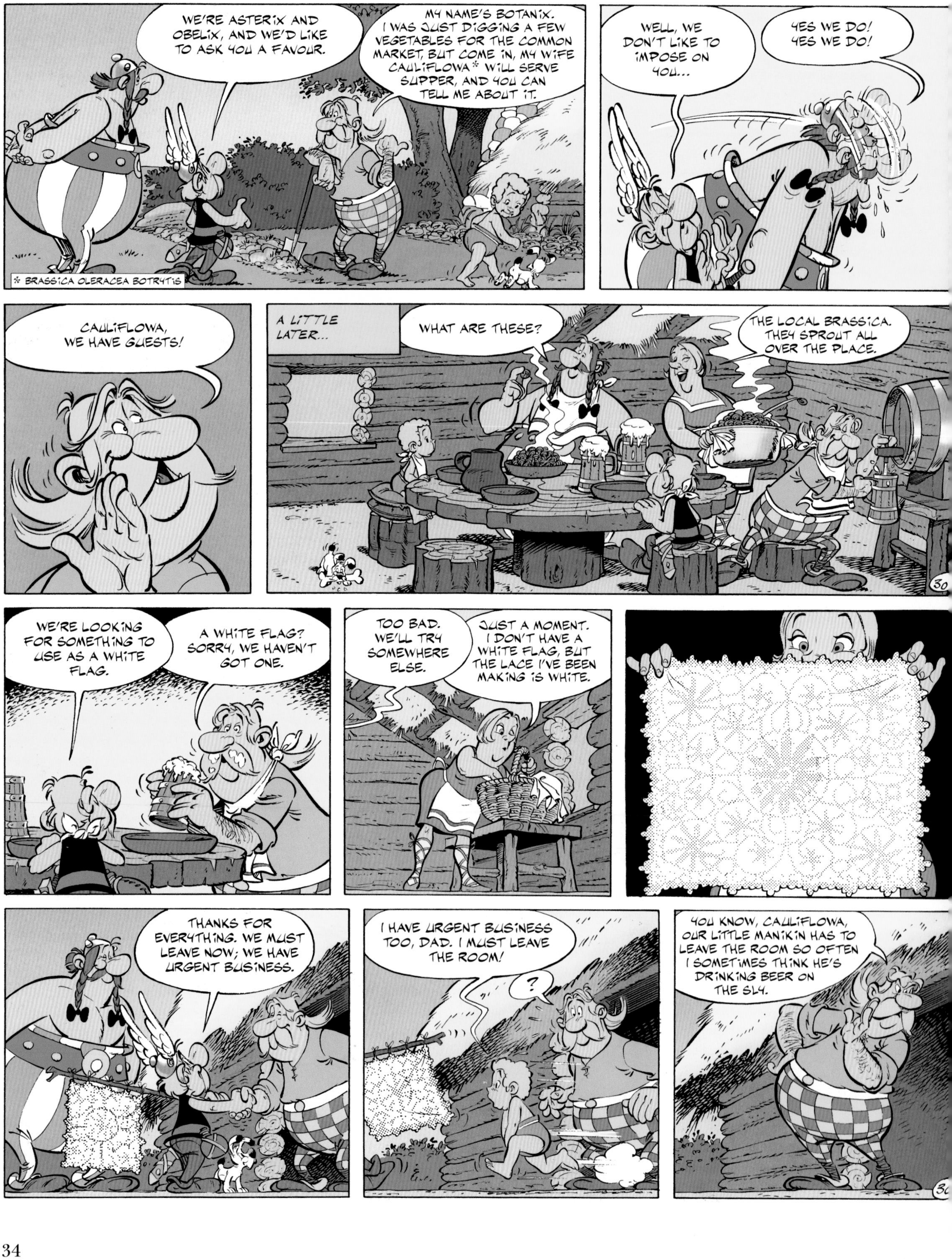
WE'RE ASTERIX AND OBELIX, AND WE'D LIKE TO ASK YOU A FAVOUR.
MY NAME'S BOTANIX. I WAS JUST DIGGING A FEW VEGETABLES FOR THE COMMON MARKET, BUT COME IN, MY WIFE CAULIFLOWA* WILL SERVE SUPPER, AND YOU CAN TELL ME ABOUT IT.
* BRASSICA OLERACEA BOTRYTIS
WELL, WE DON'T LIKE TO IMPOSE ON YOU...
YES WE DO! YES WE DO!
CAULIFLOWA, WE HAVE GUESTS!
A LITTLE LATER...
WHAT ARE THESE?
THE LOCAL BRASSICA. THEY SPROUT ALL OVER THE PLACE.
WE'RE LOOKING FOR SOMETHING TO USE AS A WHITE FLAG.
A WHITE FLAG? SORRY, WE HAVEN'T GOT ONE.
TOO BAD. WE'LL TRY SOMEWHERE ELSE.
JUST A MOMENT. I DON'T HAVE A WHITE FLAG, BUT THE LACE I'VE BEEN MAKING IS WHITE.
THANKS FOR EVERYTHING. WE MUST LEAVE NOW; WE HAVE URGENT BUSINESS.
I HAVE URGENT BUSINESS TOO, DAD. I MUST LEAVE THE ROOM!
?
YOU KNOW, CAULIFLOWA, OUR LITTLE MANIKIN HAS TO LEAVE THE ROOM SO OFTEN I SOMETIMES THINK HE'S DRINKING BEER ON THE SLY.

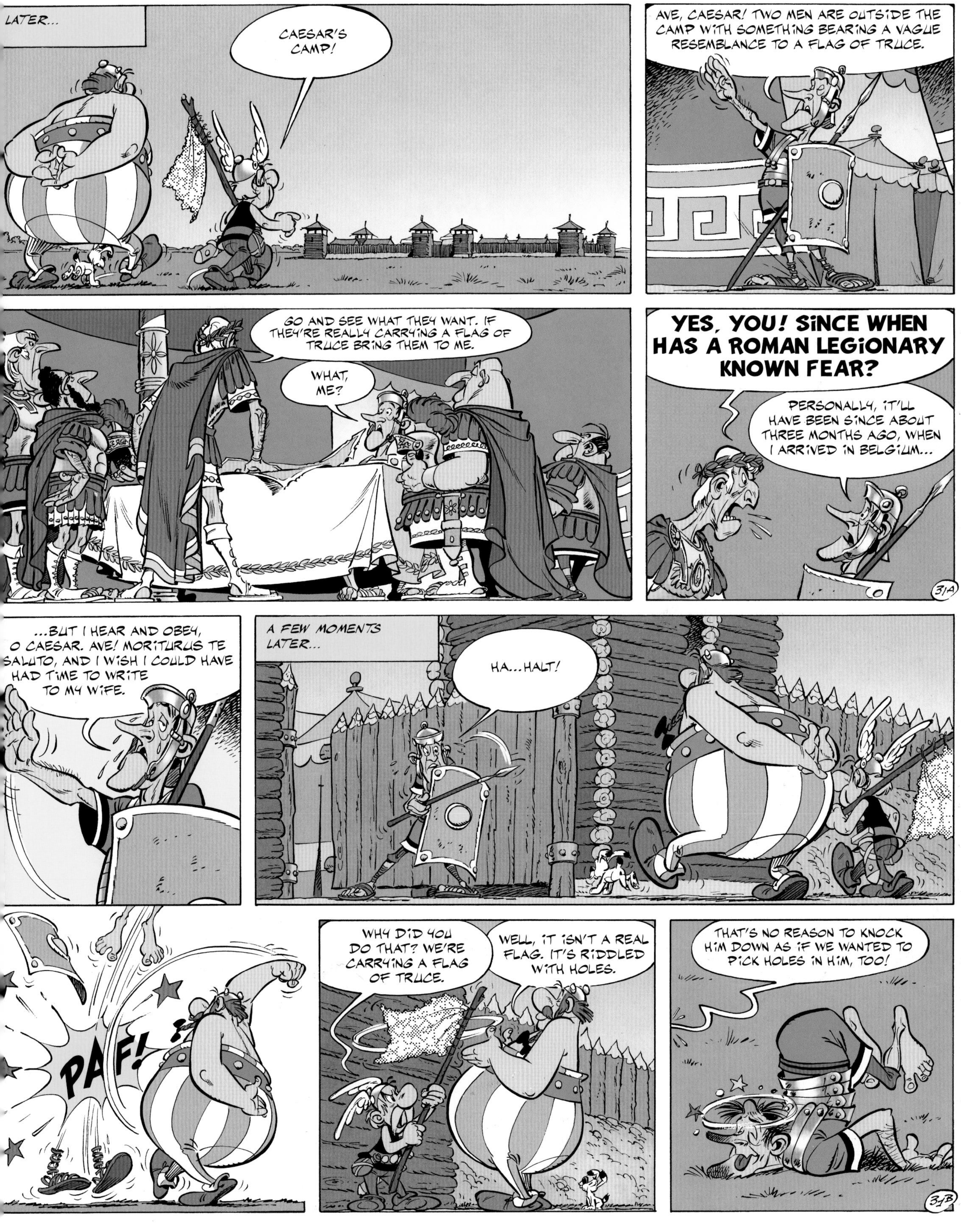
LATER...
CAESAR'S CAMP!
AVE, CAESAR! TWO MEN ARE OUTSIDE THE CAMP WITH SOMETHING BEARING A VAGUE RESEMBLANCE TO A FLAG OF TRUCE.
GO AND SEE WHAT THEY WANT. IF THEY'RE REALLY CARRYING A FLAG OF TRUCE BRING THEM TO ME.
WHAT, ME?
YES, YOU! SINCE WHEN HAS A ROMAN LEGIONARY KNOWN FEAR?
PERSONALLY, IT'LL HAVE BEEN SINCE ABOUT THREE MONTHS AGO, WHEN I ARRIVED IN BELGIUM...
...BUT I HEAR AND OBEY, O CAESAR. AVE! MORITURUS TE SALUTO, AND I WISH I COULD HAVE HAD TIME TO WRITE TO MY WIFE.
A FEW MOMENTS LATER...
HA...HALT!
PAF!
WHY DID YOU DO THAT? WE'RE CARRYING A FLAG OF TRUCE.
WELL, IT ISN'T A REAL FLAG. IT'S RIDDLED WITH HOLES.
THAT'S NO REASON TO KNOCK HIM DOWN AS IF WE WANTED TO PICK HOLES IN HIM, TOO!

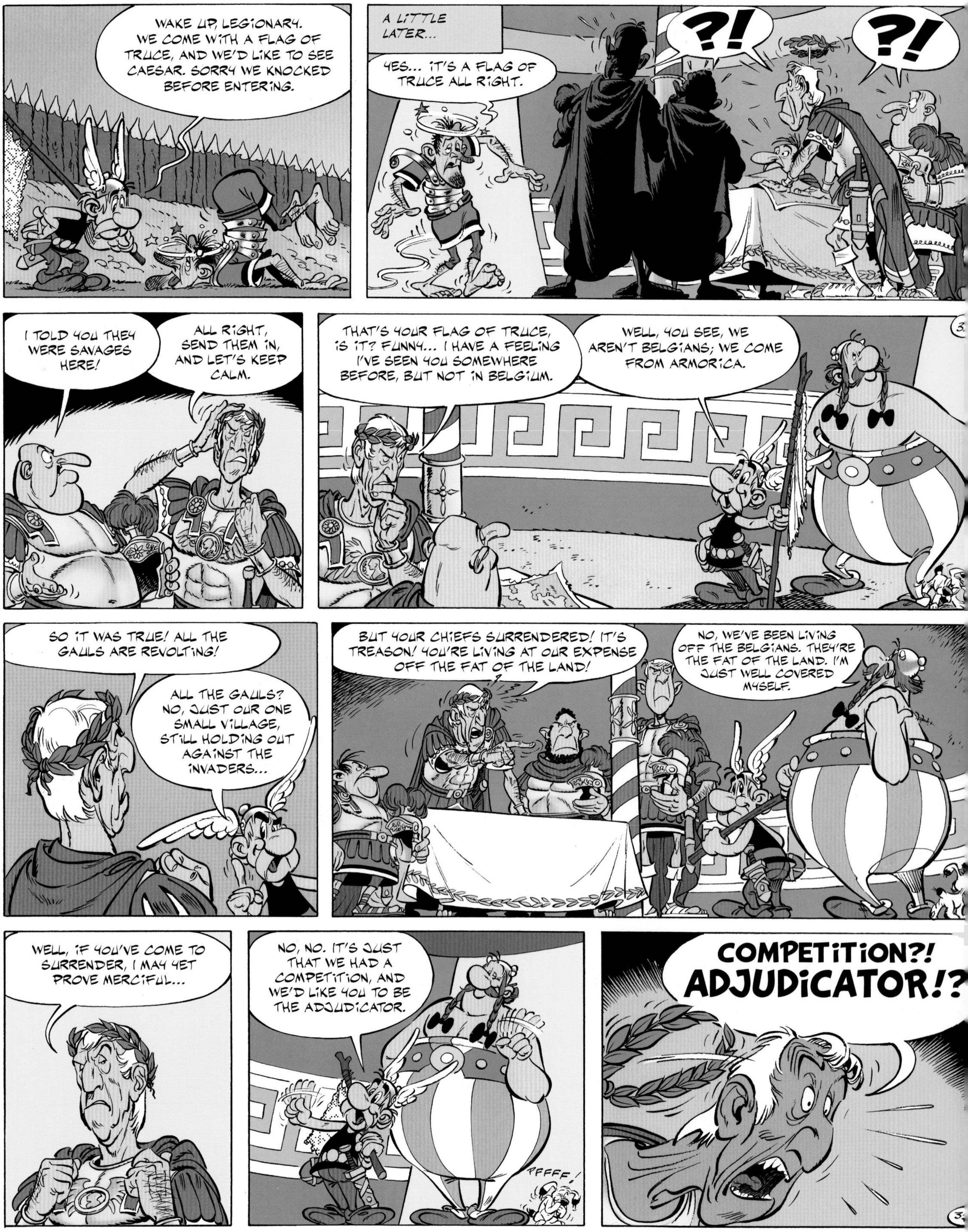
WAKE UP, LEGIONARY. WE COME WITH A FLAG OF TRUCE, AND WE'D LIKE TO SEE CAESAR. SORRY WE KNOCKED BEFORE ENTERING.
A LITTLE LATER...
YES... IT'S A FLAG OF TRUCE ALL RIGHT.
?!
?!
I TOLD YOU THEY WERE SAVAGES HERE!
ALL RIGHT, SEND THEM IN, AND LET'S KEEP CALM.
THAT'S YOUR FLAG OF TRUCE, IS IT? FUNNY... I HAVE A FEELING I'VE SEEN YOU SOMEWHERE BEFORE, BUT NOT IN BELGIUM.
WELL, YOU SEE, WE AREN'T BELGIANS; WE COME FROM ARMORICA.
SO IT WAS TRUE! ALL THE GAULS ARE REVOLTING!
ALL THE GAULS? NO, JUST OUR ONE SMALL VILLAGE, STILL HOLDING OUT AGAINST THE INVADERS...
BUT YOUR CHIEFS SURRENDERED! IT'S TREASON! YOU'RE LIVING AT OUR EXPENSE OFF THE FAT OF THE LAND!
NO, WE'VE BEEN LIVING OFF THE BELGIANS. THEY'RE THE FAT OF THE LAND. I'M JUST WELL COVERED MYSELF.
WELL, IF YOU'VE COME TO SURRENDER, I MAY YET PROVE MERCIFUL...
NO, NO. IT'S JUST THAT WE HAD A COMPETITION, AND WE'D LIKE YOU TO BE THE ADJUDICATOR.
PFFFF!
COMPETITION?! ADJUDICATOR!?

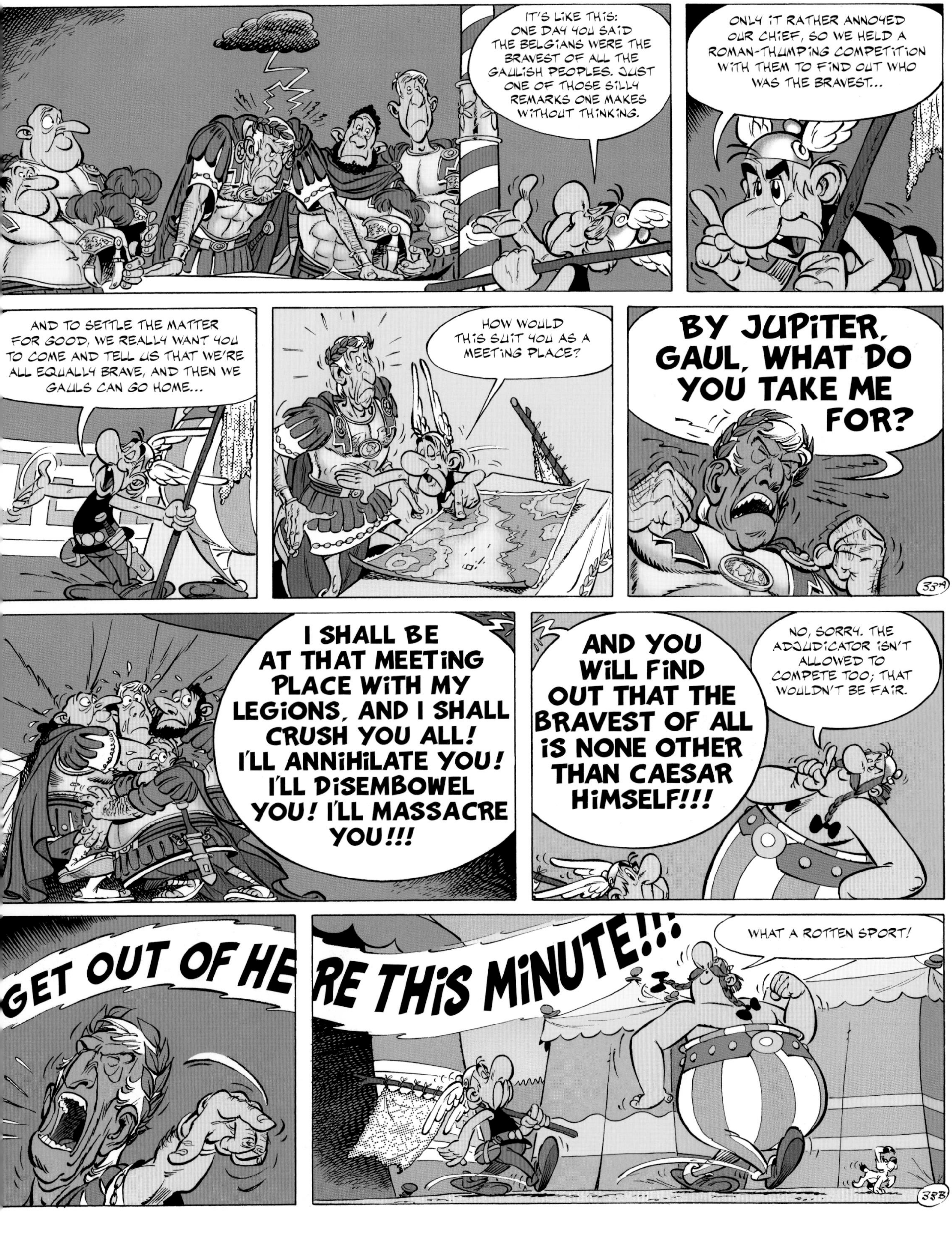

IT'S LIKE THIS: ONE DAY YOU SAID THE BELGIANS WERE THE BRAVEST OF ALL THE GAULISH PEOPLES. JUST ONE OF THOSE SILLY REMARKS ONE MAKES WITHOUT THINKING.
ONLY IT RATHER ANNOYED OUR CHIEF, SO WE HELD A ROMAN-THUMPING COMPETITION WITH THEM TO FIND OUT WHO WAS THE BRAVEST...
AND TO SETTLE THE MATTER FOR GOOD, WE REALLY WANT YOU TO COME AND TELL US THAT WE'RE ALL EQUALLY BRAVE, AND THEN WE GAULS CAN GO HOME...
HOW WOULD THIS SUIT YOU AS A MEETING PLACE?
BY JUPITER, GAUL, WHAT DO YOU TAKE ME FOR?
I SHALL BE AT THAT MEETING PLACE WITH MY LEGIONS, AND I SHALL CRUSH YOU ALL! I'LL ANNIHILATE YOU! I'LL DISEMBOWEL YOU! I'LL MASSACRE YOU!!!
AND YOU WILL FIND OUT THAT THE BRAVEST OF ALL IS NONE OTHER THAN CAESAR HIMSELF!!!
NO, SORRY. THE ADJUDICATOR ISN'T ALLOWED TO COMPETE TOO; THAT WOULDN'T BE FAIR.
GET OUT OF HERE THIS MINUTE!!!
WHAT A ROTTEN SPORT!

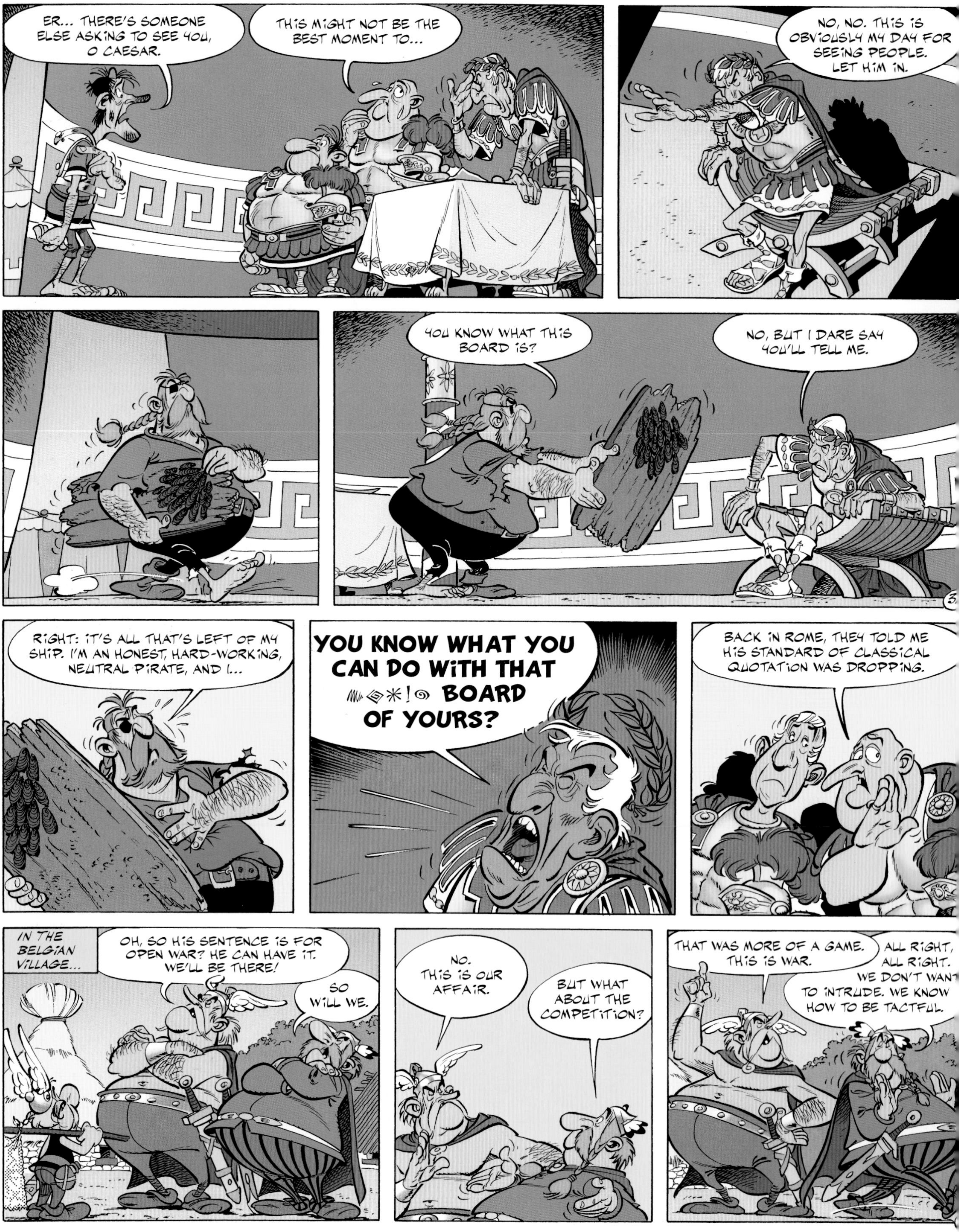

ER... THERE'S SOMEONE ELSE ASKING TO SEE YOU, O CAESAR.
THIS MIGHT NOT BE THE BEST MOMENT TO...
NO, NO. THIS IS OBVIOUSLY MY DAY FOR SEEING PEOPLE. LET HIM IN.
YOU KNOW WHAT THIS BOARD IS?
NO, BUT I DARE SAY YOU'LL TELL ME.
RIGHT: IT'S ALL THAT'S LEFT OF MY SHIP. I'M AN HONEST, HARD-WORKING, NEUTRAL PIRATE, AND I...
YOU KNOW WHAT YOU CAN DO WITH THAT !! BOARD OF YOURS?
BACK IN ROME, THEY TOLD ME HIS STANDARD OF CLASSICAL QUOTATION WAS DROPPING.
IN THE BELGIAN VILLAGE...
OH, SO HIS SENTENCE IS FOR OPEN WAR? HE CAN HAVE IT. WE'LL BE THERE!
SO WILL WE.
NO. THIS IS OUR AFFAIR.
BUT WHAT ABOUT THE COMPETITION?
THAT WAS MORE OF A GAME. THIS IS WAR.
ALL RIGHT, ALL RIGHT. WE DON'T WANT TO INTRUDE. WE KNOW HOW TO BE TACTFUL.

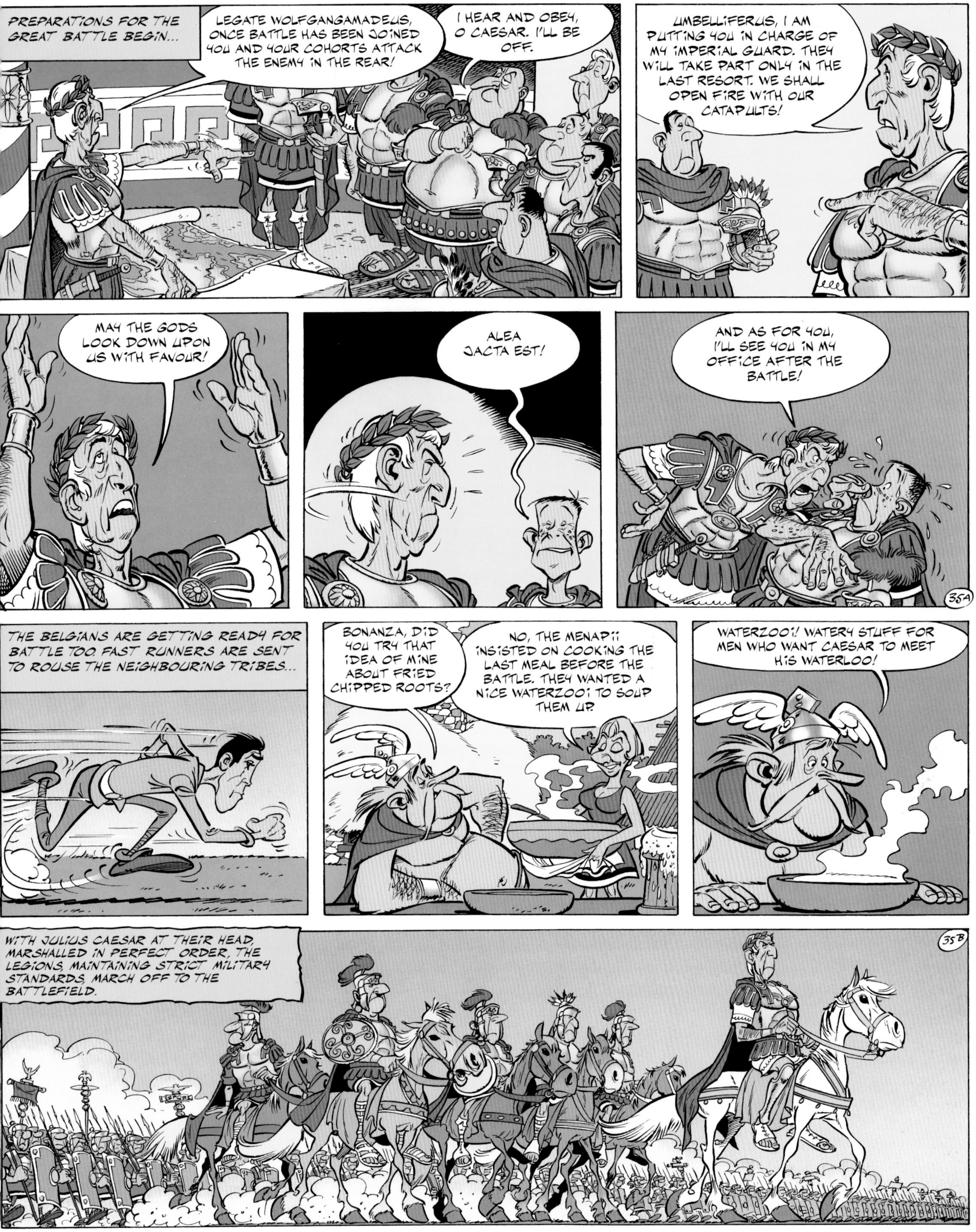
PREPARATIONS FOR THE GREAT BATTLE BEGIN...
LEGATE WOLFGANGAMADEUS, ONCE BATTLE HAS BEEN JOINED YOU AND YOUR COHORTS ATTACK THE ENEMY IN THE REAR!
I HEAR AND OBEY, O CAESAR. I'LL BE OFF.
UMBELLIFERUS, I AM PUTTING YOU IN CHARGE OF MY IMPERIAL GUARD. THEY WILL TAKE PART ONLY IN THE LAST RESORT. WE SHALL OPEN FIRE WITH OUR CATAPULTS!
MAY THE GODS LOOK DOWN UPON US WITH FAVOUR!
ALEA JACTA EST!
AND AS FOR YOU, I'LL SEE YOU IN MY OFFICE AFTER THE BATTLE!
35A
THE BELGIANS ARE GETTING READY FOR BATTLE TOO FAST RUNNERS ARE SENT TO ROUSE THE NEIGHBOURING TRIBES...
BONANZA, DID YOU TRY THAT IDEA OF MINE ABOUT FRIED CHIPPED ROOTS?
NO, THE MENAPII INSISTED ON COOKING THE LAST MEAL BEFORE THE BATTLE. THEY WANTED A NICE WATERZOOI TO SOUP THEM UP.
WATERZOOI! WATERY STUFF FOR MEN WHO WANT CAESAR TO MEET HIS WATERLOO!
WITH JULIUS CAESAR AT THEIR HEAD, MARSHALLED IN PERFECT ORDER, THE LEGIONS, MAINTAINING STRICT MILITARY STANDARDS, MARCH OFF TO THE BATTLEFIELD.
35B

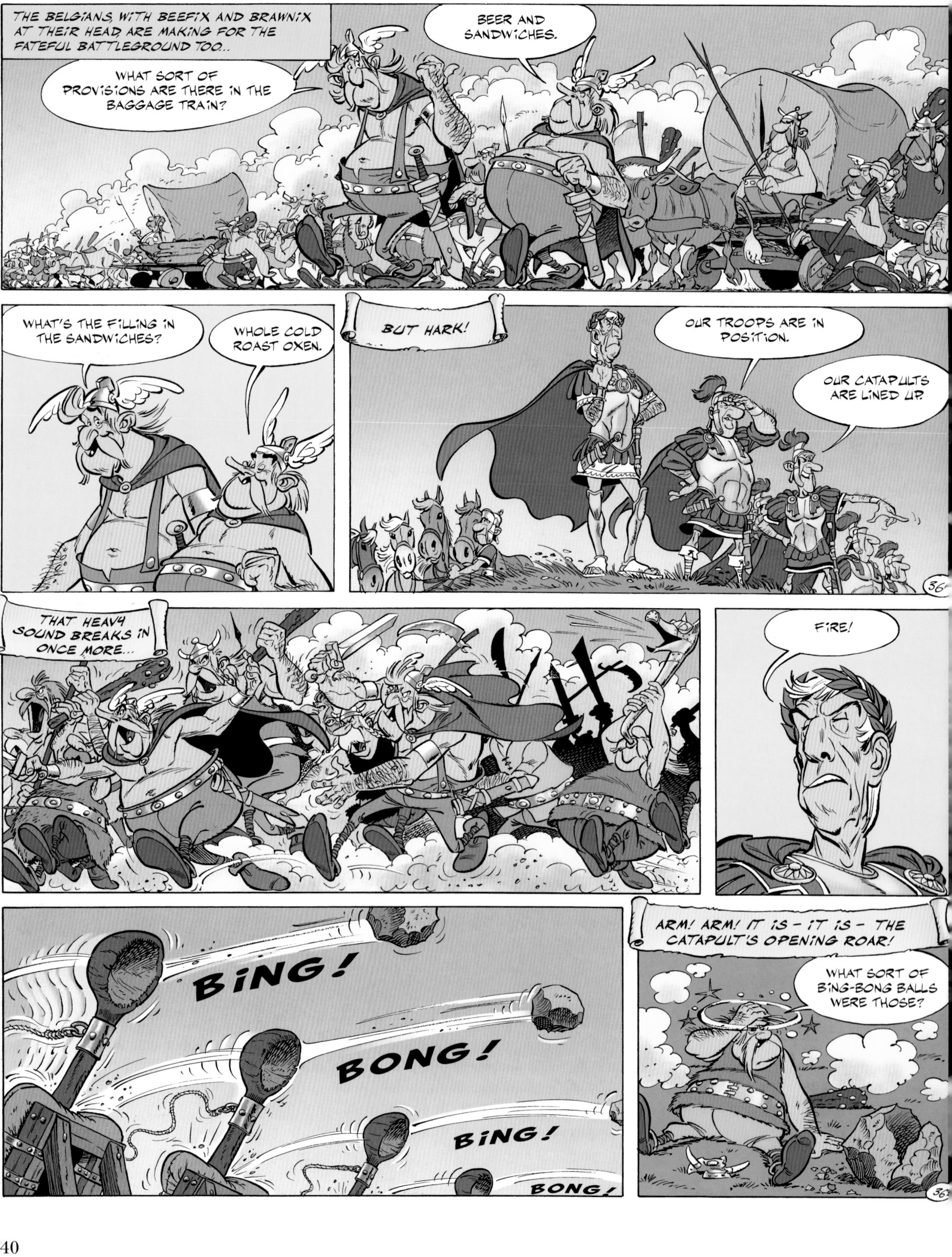
THE BELGIANS, WITH BEEFIX AND BRAWNIX AT THEIR HEAD ARE MAKING FOR THE FATEFUL BATTLEGROUND TOO...
WHAT SORT OF PROVISIONS ARE THERE IN THE BAGGAGE TRAIN?
BEER AND SANDWICHES.
WHAT'S THE FILLING IN THE SANDWICHES?
WHOLE COLD ROAST OXEN.
BUT HARK!
OUR TROOPS ARE IN POSITION.
OUR CATAPULTS ARE LINED UP.
THAT HEAVY SOUND BREAKS IN ONCE MORE...
FIRE!
BING!
BONG!
BING!
BONG!
ARM! ARM! IT IS - IT IS - THE CATAPULT'S OPENING ROAR!
WHAT SORT OF BING-BONG BALLS WERE THOSE?

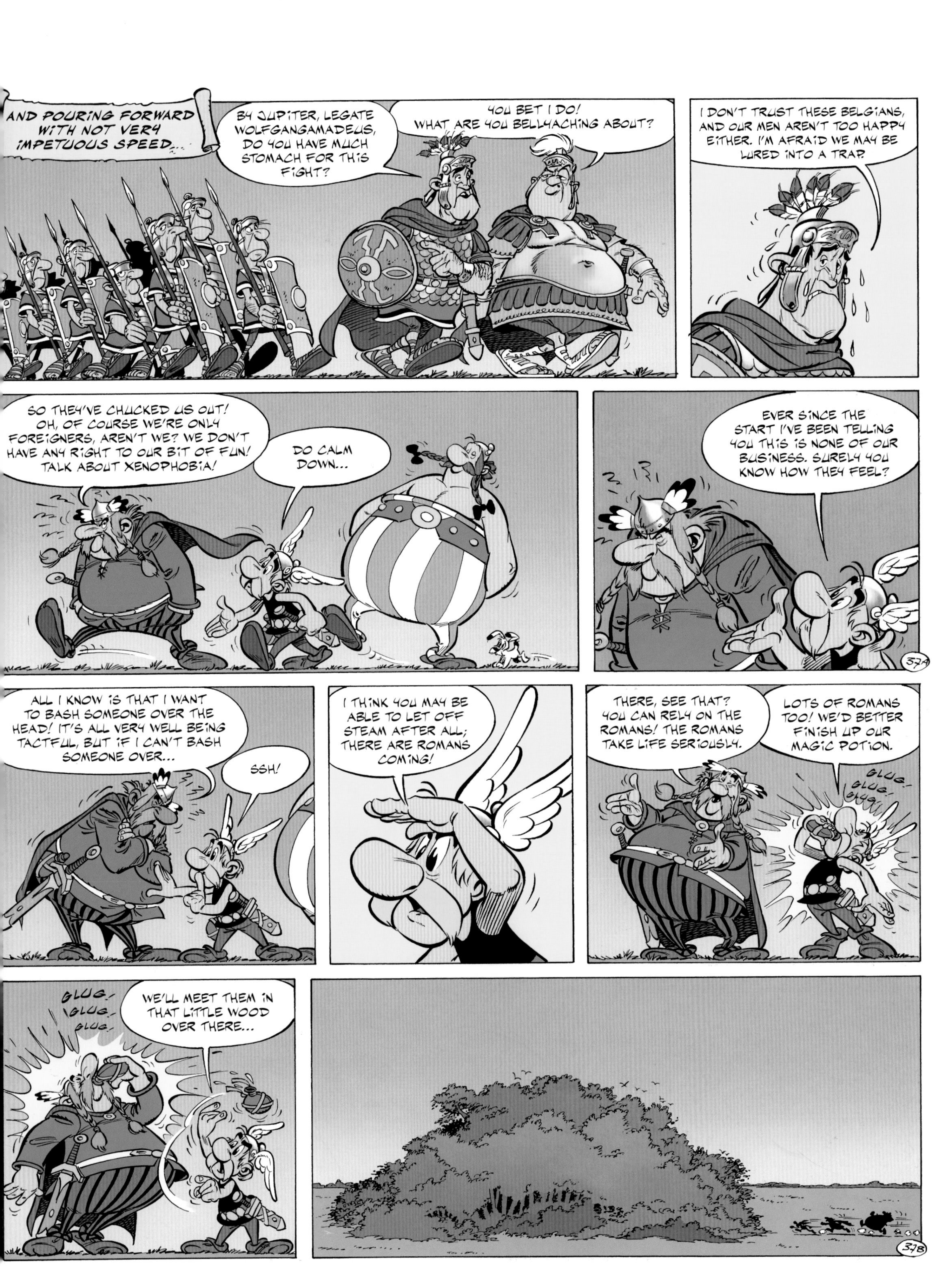
AND POURING FORWARD WITH NOT VERY IMPETUOUS SPEED...
BY JUPITER, LEGATE WOLFGANGAMADEUS, DO YOU HAVE MUCH STOMACH FOR THIS FIGHT?
YOU BET I DO! WHAT ARE YOU BELLYACHING ABOUT?
I DON'T TRUST THESE BELGIANS, AND OUR MEN AREN'T TOO HAPPY EITHER. I'M AFRAID WE MAY BE LURED INTO A TRAP.
SO THEY'VE CHUCKED US OUT! OH, OF COURSE WE'RE ONLY FOREIGNERS, AREN'T WE? WE DON'T HAVE ANY RIGHT TO OUR BIT OF FUN! TALK ABOUT XENOPHOBIA!
DO CALM DOWN...
EVER SINCE THE START I'VE BEEN TELLING YOU THIS IS NONE OF OUR BUSINESS. SURELY YOU KNOW HOW THEY FEEL?
37A
ALL I KNOW IS THAT I WANT TO BASH SOMEONE OVER THE HEAD! IT'S ALL VERY WELL BEING TACTFUL, BUT IF I CAN'T BASH SOMEONE OVER...
SSH!
I THINK YOU MAY BE ABLE TO LET OFF STEAM AFTER ALL; THERE ARE ROMANS COMING!
THERE, SEE THAT? YOU CAN RELY ON THE ROMANS! THE ROMANS TAKE LIFE SERIOUSLY.
LOTS OF ROMANS TOO! WE'D BETTER FINISH UP OUR MAGIC POTION.
GLUG, GLUG, GLUG
GLUG, GLUG, GLUG.
WE'LL MEET THEM IN THAT LITTLE WOOD OVER THERE...
37B

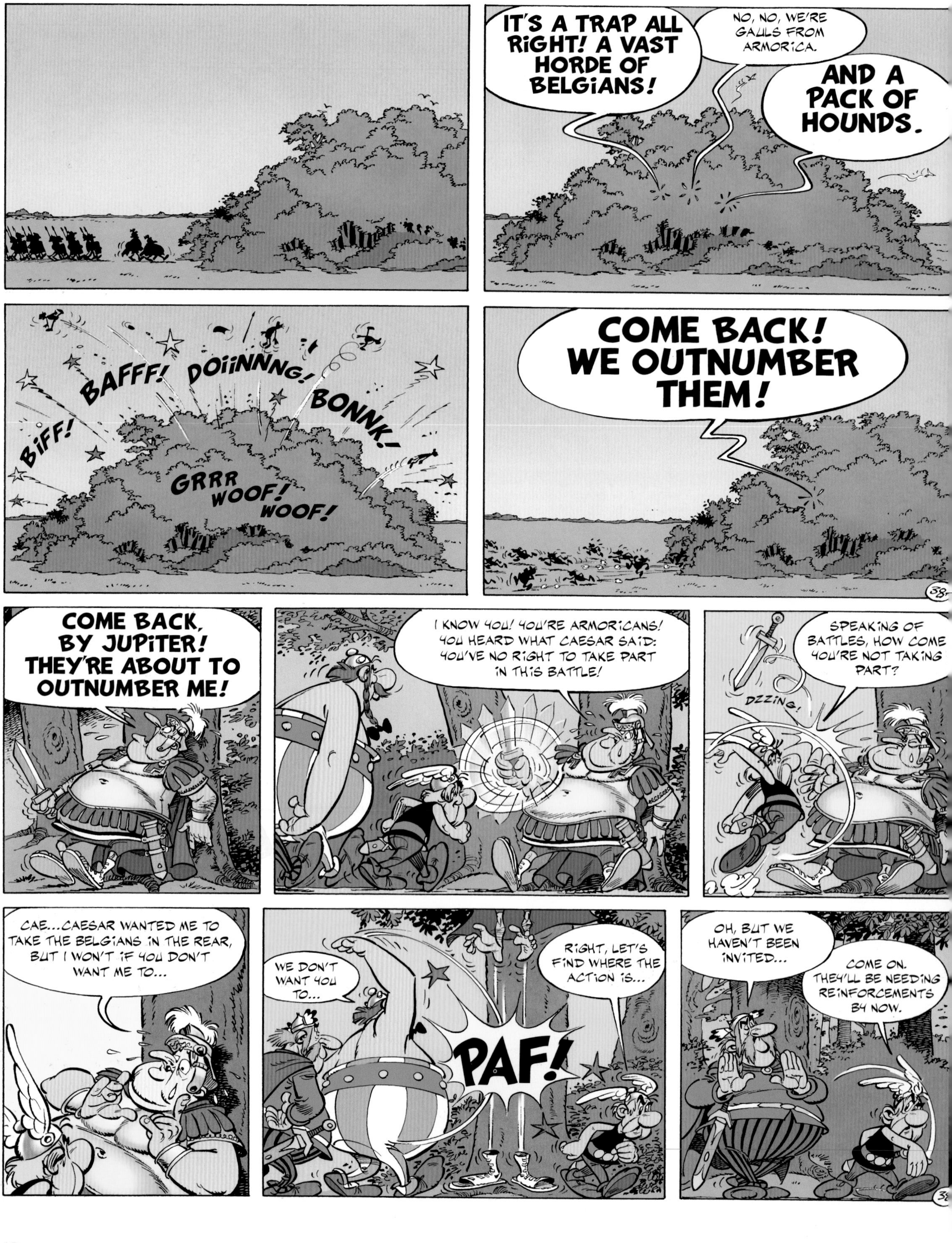
IT'S A TRAP ALL RiGHT! A VAST HORDE OF BELGiANS!
NO, NO, WE'RE GAULS FROM ARMORiCA.
AND A PACK OF HOUNDS.
BAFFF!
DOiiNNNG!
BONNK!
BiFF!
GRRR WOOF! WOOF!
COME BACK! WE OUTNUMBER THEM!
COME BACK, BY JUPiTER! THEY'RE ABOUT TO OUTNUMBER ME!
I KNOW YOU! YOU'RE ARMORiCANS! YOU HEARD WHAT CAESAR SAiD: YOU'VE NO RiGHT TO TAKE PART iN THiS BATTLE!
DZZiNG!
SPEAKiNG OF BATTLES, HOW COME YOU'RE NOT TAKiNG PART?
CAE...CAESAR WANTED ME TO TAKE THE BELGiANS iN THE REAR, BUT I WON'T iF YOU DON'T WANT ME TO...
WE DON'T WANT YOU TO...
PAF!
RiGHT, LET'S FiND WHERE THE ACTiON iS...
OH, BUT WE HAVEN'T BEEN iNViTED...
COME ON. THEY'LL BE NEEDiNG REiNFORCEMENTS BY NOW.

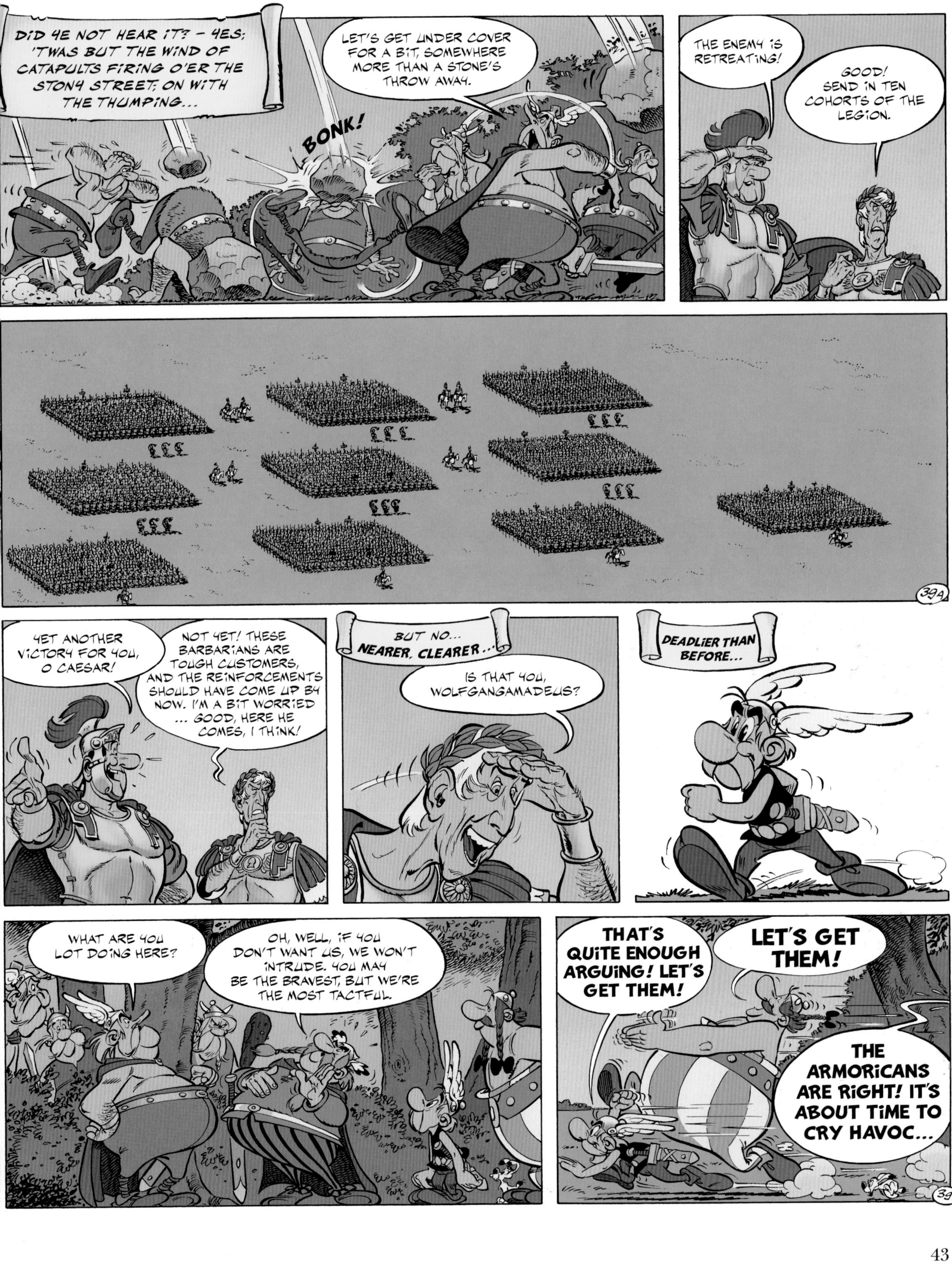
DID YE NOT HEAR IT? – YES; 'TWAS BUT THE WIND OF CATAPULTS FIRING O'ER THE STONY STREET; ON WITH THE THUMPING...
BONK!
LET'S GET UNDER COVER FOR A BIT, SOMEWHERE MORE THAN A STONE'S THROW AWAY.
THE ENEMY IS RETREATING!
GOOD! SEND IN TEN COHORTS OF THE LEGION.
YET ANOTHER VICTORY FOR YOU, O CAESAR!
NOT YET! THESE BARBARIANS ARE TOUGH CUSTOMERS, AND THE REINFORCEMENTS SHOULD HAVE COME UP BY NOW. I'M A BIT WORRIED ... GOOD, HERE HE COMES, I THINK!
BUT NO... NEARER, CLEARER...
IS THAT YOU, WOLFGANGAMADEUS?
DEADLIER THAN BEFORE...
WHAT ARE YOU LOT DOING HERE?
OH, WELL, IF YOU DON'T WANT US, WE WON'T INTRUDE. YOU MAY BE THE BRAVEST, BUT WE'RE THE MOST TACTFUL.
THAT'S QUITE ENOUGH ARGUING! LET'S GET THEM!
LET'S GET THEM!
THE ARMORICANS ARE RIGHT! IT'S ABOUT TIME TO CRY HAVOC...

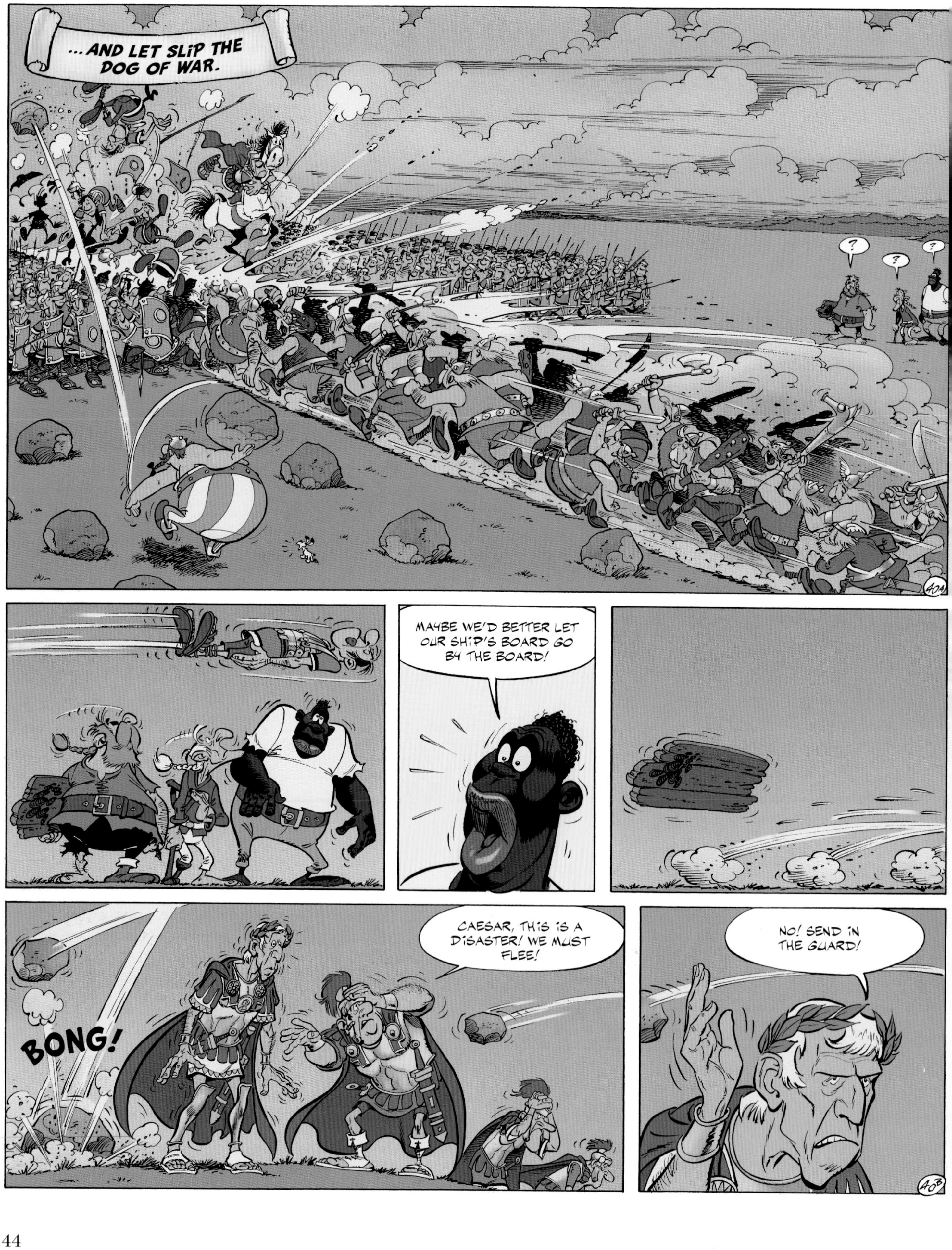

...AND LET SLIP THE DOG OF WAR.
?
?
?
MAYBE WE'D BETTER LET OUR SHIP'S BOARD GO BY THE BOARD!
BONG!
CAESAR, THIS IS A DISASTER! WE MUST FLEE!
NO! SEND IN THE GUARD!

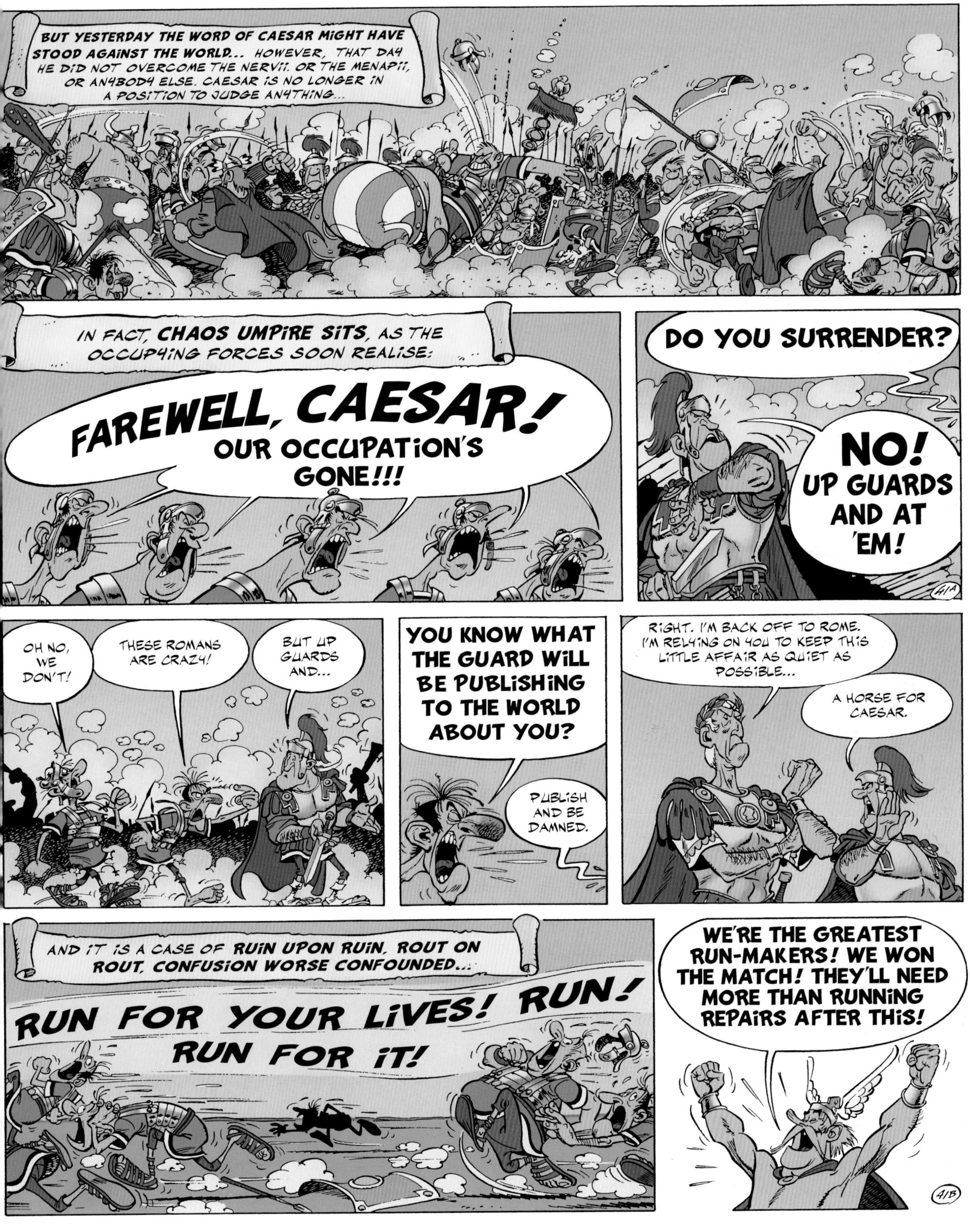
BUT YESTERDAY THE WORD OF CAESAR MIGHT HAVE STOOD AGAINST THE WORLD... HOWEVER, THAT DAY HE DID NOT OVERCOME THE NERVII OR THE MENAPII, OR ANYBODY ELSE. CAESAR IS NO LONGER IN A POSITION TO JUDGE ANYTHING...
IN FACT, CHAOS UMPIRE SITS, AS THE OCCUPYING FORCES SOON REALISE:
FAREWELL, CAESAR! OUR OCCUPATION'S GONE!!!
DO YOU SURRENDER?
NO! UP GUARDS AND AT 'EM!
OH NO, WE DON'T!
THESE ROMANS ARE CRAZY!
BUT UP GUARDS AND...
YOU KNOW WHAT THE GUARD WILL BE PUBLISHING TO THE WORLD ABOUT YOU?
PUBLISH AND BE DAMNED.
RIGHT. I'M BACK OFF TO ROME. I'M RELYING ON YOU TO KEEP THIS LITTLE AFFAIR AS QUIET AS POSSIBLE...
A HORSE FOR CAESAR.
AND IT IS A CASE OF RUIN UPON RUIN, ROUT ON ROUT, CONFUSION WORSE CONFOUNDED...
RUN FOR YOUR LIVES! RUN! RUN FOR IT!
WE'RE THE GREATEST RUN-MAKERS! WE WON THE MATCH! THEY'LL NEED MORE THAN RUNNING REPAIRS AFTER THIS!

THE WAY'S BARRED.

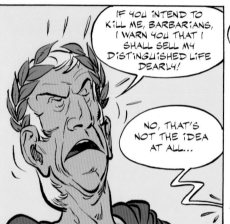

IF YOU INTEND TO KILL ME, BARBARIANS, I WARN YOU THAT I SHALL SELL MY DISTINGUISHED LIFE DEARLY!

NO, THAT'S NOT THE IDEA AT ALL...

IT'S ABOUT OUR COMPETITION...

YOU'VE SEEN US IN ACTION, SO NOW WILL YOU ADJUDICATE? WHO ARE THE BRAVEST?

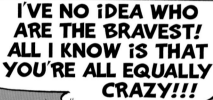

I'VE NO IDEA WHO ARE THE BRAVEST! ALL I KNOW IS THAT YOU'RE ALL EQUALLY CRAZY!!!

AND NOW I'M GOING BACK TO ROME, AND I DON'T WANT TO BE BOTHERED ANY MORE! OFF WE GO!

? !

PFFFFFF

PFFFFFF

HAHAHA! HOHOHO!

COME ON BACK TO THE VILLAGE, AND WE'LL HAVE A LITTLE PARTY TO CELEBRATE!

WHAT ON EARTH IS THAT?

NO IDEA... A SOUVENIR I PICKED UP ON THE BATTLEFIELD!

LOOKS LIKE A SEASIDE SOUVENIR ... IT EVEN HAS MUSSELS STILL STICKING TO IT.

MUSSELS... THAT'S FISHY... FISH... WONDER HOW FISH WOULD GO WITH CHIPPED ROOT VEGETABLES?

AND THERE IS A SOUND OF REVELRY BY NIGHT.

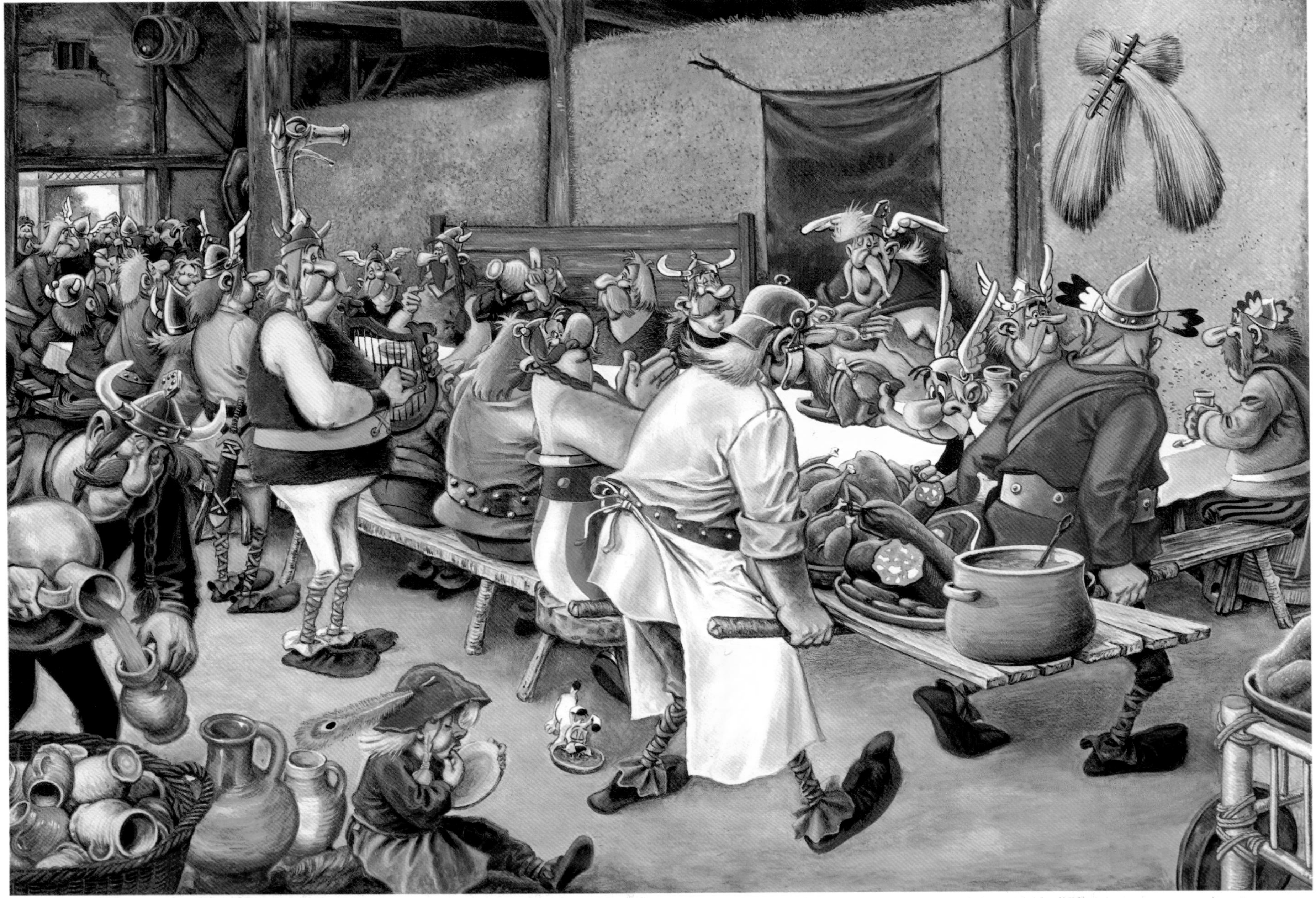

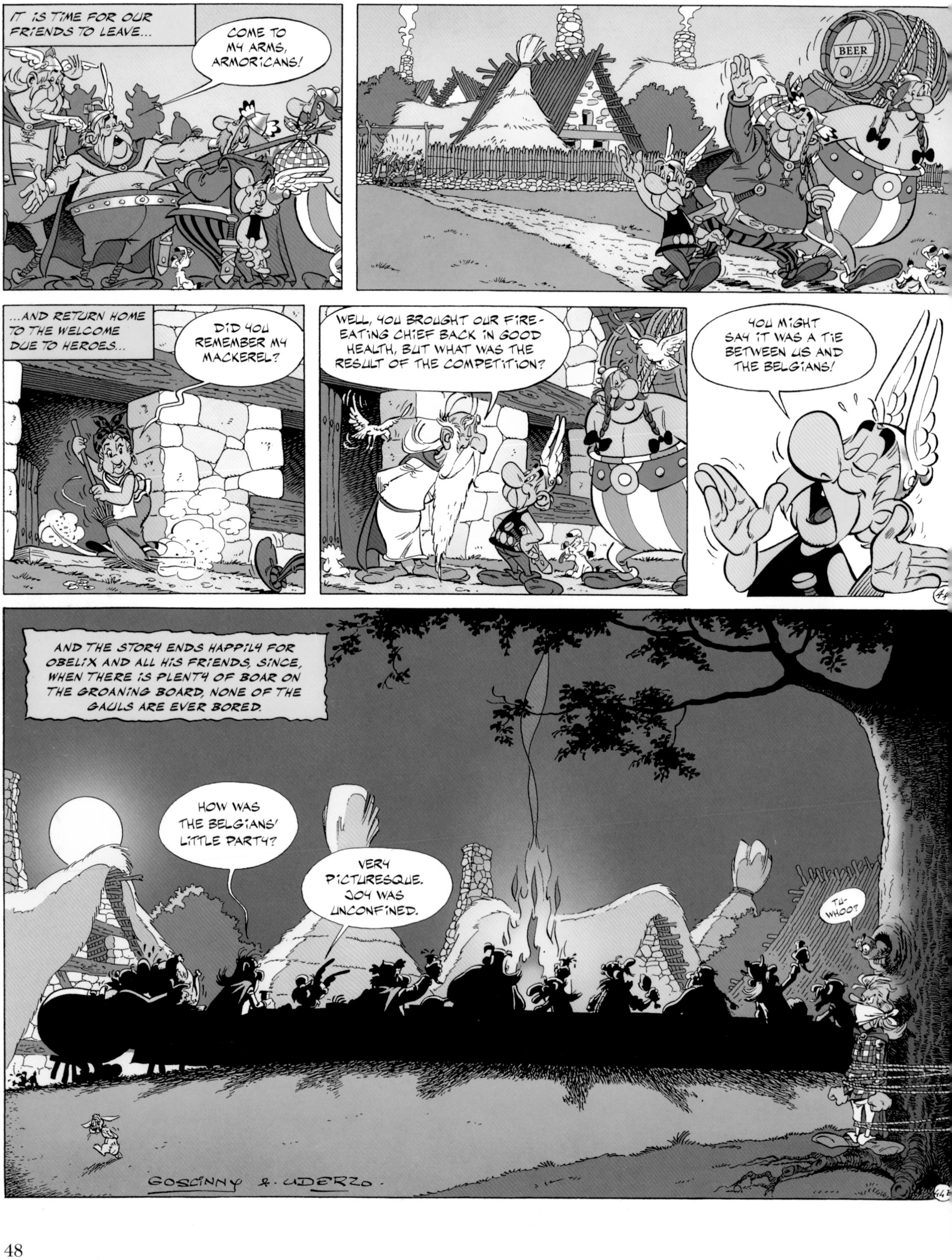
IT IS TIME FOR OUR FRIENDS TO LEAVE...
COME TO MY ARMS, ARMORICANS!
BEER
...AND RETURN HOME TO THE WELCOME DUE TO HEROES...
DID YOU REMEMBER MY MACKEREL?
WELL, YOU BROUGHT OUR FIRE-EATING CHIEF BACK IN GOOD HEALTH, BUT WHAT WAS THE RESULT OF THE COMPETITION?
YOU MIGHT SAY IT WAS A TIE BETWEEN US AND THE BELGIANS!
AND THE STORY ENDS HAPPILY FOR OBELIX AND ALL HIS FRIENDS, SINCE, WHEN THERE IS PLENTY OF BOAR ON THE GROANING BOARD, NONE OF THE GAULS ARE EVER BORED.
HOW WAS THE BELGIANS' LITTLE PARTY?
VERY PICTURESQUE. JOY WAS UNCONFINED.
TU-WHOO?
GOSCINNY & UDERZO.